Godfrey Morgan

A Californian Mystery

Jules Verne

Godfrey Morgan: A Californian Mystery

The present edition is a reproduction of previous publication of this classic work. Minor typographical errors may have been corrected without note; however, for an authentic reading experience the spelling, punctuation, and capitalization have been retained from the original text.

ISBN: 978-1-63637-174-0

CONTENTS

CHAPTER I

IN WHICH THE READER HAS THE OPPORTUNITY OF BUYING AN ISLAND IN THE PACIFIC OCEAN

"An island to sell, for cash, to the highest bidder!" said Dean Felporg, the auctioneer, standing behind his rostrum in the room where the conditions of the singular sale were being noisily discussed.

"Island for sale! island for sale!" repeated in shrill tones again and again Gingrass, the crier, who was threading his way in and out of the excited crowd closely packed inside the largest saloon in the auction mart at No. 10, Sacramento Street.

The crowd consisted not only of a goodly number of Americans from the States of Utah, Oregon, and California, but also of a few Frenchmen, who form quite a sixth of the population.

Mexicans were there enveloped in their sarapes; Chinamen in their large-sleeved tunics, pointed shoes, and conical hats; one or two Kanucks from the coast; and even a sprinkling of Black Feet, Grosventres, or Flatheads, from the banks of the Trinity river.

The scene is in San Francisco, the capital of California, but not at the period when the placer-mining fever was raging—from 1849 to 1852. San Francisco was no longer what it had been then, a caravanserai, a terminus, an *inn*, where for a night there slept the busy men who were hastening to the gold-fields west of the Sierra Nevada. At the end of some twenty years the old unknown Yerba-Buena had given place to a town unique of its kind, peopled by 100,000 inhabitants, built under the shelter of a couple of hills, away from the shore, but stretching off to the farthest heights in the background—a city in short which has dethroned Lima, Santiago, Valparaiso, and every other rival, and which the Americans have made the queen of the Pacific, the "glory of the western coast!"

It was the 15th of May, and the weather was still cold. In California, subject as it is to the direct action of the polar currents, the first weeks of this month are somewhat similar to the last weeks of March in Central Europe. But the cold was hardly noticeable in the thick of the auction crowd. The bell with its incessant clangour had brought together an enormous throng, and quite a summer temperature caused the drops of perspiration to glisten on the foreheads of the spectators which the cold outside would have soon solidified.

1

Do not imagine that all these folks had come to the auction-room with the intention of buying. I might say that all of them had but come to see. Who was going to be mad enough, even if he were rich enough, to purchase an isle of the Pacific, which the government had in some eccentric moment decided to sell? Would the reserve price ever be reached? Could anybody be found to work up the bidding? If not, it would scarcely be the fault of the public crier, who tried his best to tempt buyers by his shoutings and gestures, and the flowery metaphors of his harangue. People laughed at him, but they did not seem much influenced by him.

"An island! an isle to sell!" repeated Gingrass.

"But not to buy!" answered an Irishman, whose pocket did not hold enough to pay for a single pebble.

"An island which at the valuation will not fetch six dollars an acre!" said the auctioneer.

"And which won't pay an eighth per cent.!" replied a big farmer, who was well acquainted with agricultural speculations.

"An isle which measures quite sixty-four miles round and has an area of two hundred and twenty-five thousand acres!"

"Is it solid on its foundation?" asked a Mexican, an old customer at the liquor-bars, whose personal solidity seemed rather doubtful at the moment.

"An isle with forests still virgin!" repeated the crier, "with prairies, hills, watercourses—"

"Warranted?" asked a Frenchman, who seemed rather inclined to nibble.

"Yes! warranted!" added Felporg, much too old at his trade to be moved by the chaff of the public.

"For two years?"

"To the end of the world!"

"Beyond that?"

"A freehold island!" repeated the crier, "an island without a single noxious animal, no wild beasts, no reptiles!—"

"No birds?" added a wag.

"No insects?" inquired another.

"An island for the highest bidder!" said Dean Felporg, beginning again. "Come, gentlemen, come! Have a little courage in your pockets! Who wants an island in perfect state of repair, never been used, an island in the Pacific, that ocean of oceans? The valuation is a mere nothing! It is put at eleven hundred thousand dollars, is there any one will bid? Who speaks first? You, sir?—you, over there nodding your head like a porcelain mandarin? Here is an island! a really good island! Who says an island?"

2

"Pass it round!" said a voice as if they were dealing with a picture or a vase.

And the room shouted with laughter, but not a half-dollar was bid.

However, if the lot could not be passed round, the map of the island was at the public disposal. The whereabouts of the portion of the globe under consideration could be accurately ascertained. There was neither surprise nor disappointment to be feared in that respect. Situation, orientation, outline, altitudes, levels, hydrography, climatology, lines of communication, all these were easily to be verified in advance. People were not buying a pig in a poke, and most undoubtedly there could be no mistake as to the nature of the goods on sale. Moreover, the innumerable journals of the United States, especially those of California, with their dailies, bi-weeklies, weeklies, bi-monthlies, monthlies, their reviews, magazines, bulletins, &c., had been for several months directing constant attention to the island whose sale by auction had been authorized by Act of Congress.

The island was Spencer Island, which lies in the west-south-west of the Bay of San Francisco, about 460 miles from the Californian coast, in 32° 15' north latitude, and 145° 18' west longitude, reckoning from Greenwich. It would be impossible to imagine a more isolated position, quite out of the way of all maritime or commercial traffic, although Spencer Island was relatively, not very far off, and situated practically in American waters. But thereabouts the regular currents diverging to the north and south have formed a kind of lake of calms, which is sometimes known as the "Whirlpool of Fleurieu."

It is in the centre of this enormous eddy, which has hardly an appreciable movement, that Spencer Island is situated. And so it is sighted by very few ships. The main routes of the Pacific, which join the new to the old continent, and lead away to China or Japan, run in a more southerly direction. Sailing-vessels would meet with endless calms in the Whirlpool of Fleurieu; and steamers, which always take the shortest road, would gain no advantage by crossing it. Hence ships of neither class know anything of Spencer Island, which rises above the waters like the isolated summit of one of the submarine mountains of the Pacific. Truly, for a man wishing to flee from the noise of the world, seeking quiet in solitude, what could be better than this island, lost within a few hundred miles of the coast? For a voluntary Robinson Crusoe, it would be the very ideal of its kind! Only of course he must pay for it.

And now, why did the United States desire to part with the

island? Was it for some whim? No! A great nation cannot act on caprice in any matter, however simple. The truth was this: situated as it was, Spencer Island had for a long time been known as a station perfectly useless. There could be no practical result from settling there. In a military point of view it was of no importance, for it only commanded an absolutely deserted portion of the Pacific. In a commercial point of view there was a similar want of importance, for the products would not pay the freight either inwards or outwards. For a criminal colony it was too far from the coast. And to occupy it in any way, would be a very expensive undertaking. So it had remained deserted from time immemorial, and Congress, composed of "eminently practical" men, had resolved to put it up for sale—on one condition only, and that was, that its purchaser should be a free American citizen. There was no intention of giving away the island for nothing, and so the reserve price had been fixed at $1,100,000. This amount for a financial society dealing with such matters was a mere bagatelle, if the transaction could offer any advantages; but as we need hardly repeat, it offered none, and competent men attached no more value to this detached portion of the United States, than to one of the islands lost beneath the glaciers of the Pole.

In one sense, however, the amount was considerable. A man must be rich to pay for this hobby, for in any case it would not return him a halfpenny per cent. He would even have to be immensely rich for the transaction was to be a "cash" one, and even in the United States it is as yet rare to find citizens with $1,100,000 in their pockets, who would care to throw them into the water without hope of return.

And Congress had decided not to sell the island under the price. Eleven hundred thousand dollars, not a cent less, or Spencer Island would remain the property of the Union.

It was hardly likely that any one would be mad enough to buy it on the terms.

Besides, it was expressly reserved that the proprietor, if one offered, should not become king of Spencer Island, but president of a republic. He would gain no right to have subjects, but only fellow-citizens, who could elect him for a fixed time, and would be free from re-electing him indefinitely. Under any circumstances he was forbidden to play at monarchy. The Union could never tolerate the foundation of a kingdom, no matter how small, in American waters.

This reservation was enough to keep off many an ambitious millionaire, many an aged nabob, who might like to compete with

4

the kings of the Sandwich, the Marquesas, and the other archipelagoes of the Pacific.

In short, for one reason or other, nobody presented himself. Time was getting on, the crier was out of breath in his efforts to secure a buyer, the auctioneer orated without obtaining a single specimen of those nods which his estimable fraternity are so quick to discover; and the reserve price was not even mentioned.

However, if the hammer was not wearied with oscillating above the rostrum, the crowd was not wearied with waiting around it. The joking continued to increase, and the chaff never ceased for a moment. One individual offered two dollars for the island, costs included. Another said that a man ought to be paid that for taking it.

And all the time the crier was heard with,—

"An island to sell! an island for sale!"

And there was no one to buy it.

"Will you guarantee that there are flats there?" said Stumpy, the grocer of Merchant Street, alluding to the deposits so famous in alluvial gold-mining.

"No," answered the auctioneer, "but it is not impossible that there are, and the State abandons all its rights over the gold lands."

"Haven't you got a volcano?" asked Oakhurst, the bar-keeper of Montgomery Street.

"No volcanoes," replied Dean Felporg, "if there were, we could not sell at this price!"

An immense shout of laughter followed.

"An island to sell! an island for sale!" yelled Gingrass, whose lungs tired themselves out to no purpose.

"Only a dollar! only a half-dollar! only a cent above the reserve!" said the auctioneer for the last time, "and I will knock it down! Once! Twice!"

Perfect silence.

"If nobody bids we must put the lot back! Once! Twice!

"Twelve hundred thousand dollars!"

The four words rang through the room like four shots from a revolver.

The crowd, suddenly speechless, turned towards the bold man who had dared to bid.

It was William W. Kolderup, of San Francisco.

5

CHAPTER II

HOW WILLIAM W. KOLDERUP, OF SAN FRANCISCO, WAS AT LOGGERHEADS WITH J. R. TASKINAR, OF STOCKTON

A man extraordinarily rich, who counted dollars by the million as other men do by the thousand; such was William W. Kolderup.

People said he was richer than the Duke of Westminster, whose income is some $4,000,000 a year, and who can spend his $10,000 a day, or seven dollars every minute; richer than Senator Jones, of Nevada, who has $35,000,000 in the funds; richer than Mr. Mackay himself, whose annual $13,750,000 give him $1560 per hour, or half-a-dollar to spend every second of his life.

I do not mention such minor millionaires as the Rothschilds, the Vanderbilts, the Dukes of Northumberland, or the Stewarts, nor the directors of the powerful bank of California, and other opulent personages of the old and new worlds whom William W. Kolderup would have been able to comfortably pension. He could, without inconvenience, have given away a million just as you and I might give away a shilling.

It was in developing the early placer-mining enterprises in California that our worthy speculator had laid the solid foundations of his incalculable fortune. He was the principal associate of Captain Sutter, the Swiss, in the localities, where, in 1848, the first traces were discovered. Since then, luck and shrewdness combined had helped him on, and he had interested himself in all the great enterprises of both worlds. He threw himself boldly into commercial and industrial speculations. His inexhaustible funds were the life of hundreds of factories, his ships were on every sea. His wealth increased not in arithmetical but in geometrical progression. People spoke of him as one of those few "milliardaires" who never know how much they are worth. In reality he knew almost to a dollar, but he never boasted of it.

At this very moment when we introduce him to our readers with all the consideration such a many-sided man merits, William W. Kolderup had 2000 branch offices scattered over the globe, 80,000 employés in America, Europe, and Australia, 300,000 correspondents, a fleet of 500 ships which continually ploughed the ocean for his profit, and he was spending not less than a million a year in bill-stamps and postages. In short, he was the honour and glory of opulent Frisco—the nickname familiarly given by the Americans to the Californian capital.

A bid from William W. Kolderup could not but be a serious one. And when the crowd in the auction room had recognized who it was that by $100,000 had capped the reserve price of Spencer Island, there was an irresistible sensation, the chaffing ceased instantly, jokes gave place to interjections of admiration, and cheers resounded through the saloon. Then a deep silence succeeded to the hubbub, eyes grew bigger, and ears opened wider. For our part had we been there we would have had to hold our breath that we might lose nothing of the exciting scene which would follow should any one dare to bid against William W. Kolderup.

But was it probable? Was it even possible?

No! And at the outset it was only necessary to look at William W. Kolderup to feel convinced that he could never yield on a question where his financial gallantry was at stake.

He was a big, powerful man, with huge head, large shoulders, well-built limbs, firmly knit, and tough as iron. His quiet but resolute look was not willingly cast downwards, his grey hair, brushed up in front, was as abundant as if he were still young. The straight lines of his nose formed a geometrically-drawn right-angled triangle. No moustache; his beard cut in Yankee fashion bedecked his chin, and the two upper points met at the opening of the lips and ran up to the temples in pepper-and-salt whiskers; teeth of snowy whiteness were symmetrically placed on the borders of a clean-cut mouth. The head of one of those true kings of men who rise in the tempest and face the storm. No hurricane could bend that head, so solid was the neck which supported it. In these battles of the bidders each of its nods meant an additional hundred thousand dollars.

There was no one to dispute with him.

"Twelve hundred thousand dollars—twelve hundred thousand!" said the auctioneer, with that peculiar accent which men of his vocation find most effective.

"Going at twelve hundred thousand dollars!" repeated Gingrass the crier.

"You could safely bid more than that," said Oakhurst, the barkeeper; "William Kolderup will never give in."

"He knows no one will chance it," answered the grocer from Merchant Street.

Repeated cries of "Hush!" told the two worthy tradesmen to be quiet. All wished to hear. All hearts palpitated. Dare any one raise his voice in answer to the voice of William W. Kolderup? He, magnificent to look upon, never moved. There he remained as calm

7

as if the matter had no interest for him. But—and this those near to him noticed—his eyes were like revolvers loaded with dollars, ready to fire.

"Nobody speaks?" asked Dean Felporg.

Nobody spoke.

"Once! Twice!"

"Once! Twice!" repeated Gingrass, quite accustomed to this little dialogue with his chief.

"Going!"

"Going!"

"For twelve—hundred—thousand—dollars—Spencer—Island—com—plete!"

"For twelve—hundred—thousand—dollars!"

"That is so? No mistake?"

"No withdrawal?"

"For twelve hundred thousand dollars, Spencer Island!"

The waistcoats rose and fell convulsively. Could it be possible that at the last second a higher bid would come? Felporg with his right hand stretched on the table was shaking his ivory hammer—one rap, two raps, and the deed would be done.

The public could not have been more absorbed in the face of a summary application of the law of Justice Lynch!

The hammer slowly fell, almost touched the table, rose again, hovered an instant like a sword which pauses ere the drawer cleaves the victim in twain; then it flashed swiftly downwards.

But before the sharp rap could be given, a voice was heard giving utterance to these four words,—

"Thirteen—hundred—thousand—dollars!"

There was a preliminary "Ah!" of general stupefaction, then a second "Ah!" of not less general satisfaction. Another bidder had presented himself! There was going to be a fight after all!

But who was the reckless individual who had dared to come to dollar strokes with William W. Kolderup of San Francisco?

It was J. R. Taskinar, of Stockton.

J. R. Taskinar was rich, but he was more than proportionately fat. He weighed 490 lbs. If he had only run second in the last fat-man show at Chicago, it was because he had not been allowed time to finish his dinner, and had lost about a dozen pounds.

This colossus, who had had to have special chairs made for his portly person to rest upon, lived at Stockton, on the San Joachim. Stockton is one of the most important cities in California, one of the depôt centres for the mines of the south, the rival of Sacramento the

8

centre for the mines of the north. There the ships embark the largest quantity of Californian corn.

Not only had the development of the mines and speculations in wheat furnished J. R. Taskinar with the occasion of gaining an enormous fortune, but petroleum, like another Pactolus, had run through his treasury. Besides, he was a great gambler, a lucky gambler, and he had found "poker" most prodigal of its favours to him.

But if he was a Crœsus, he was also a rascal; and no one would have addressed him as "honourable," although the title in those parts is so much in vogue. After all, he was a good war-horse, and perhaps more was put on his back than was justly his due. One thing was certain, and that was that on many an occasion he had not hesitated to use his "Derringer"—the Californian revolver.

Now J. R. Taskinar particularly detested William W. Kolderup. He envied him for his wealth, his position, and his reputation. He despised him as a fat man despises a lean one. It was not the first time that the merchant of Stockton had endeavoured to do the merchant of San Francisco out of some business or other, good or bad, simply owing to a feeling of rivalry. William W. Kolderup thoroughly knew his man, and on all occasions treated him with scorn enough to drive him to distraction.

The last success which J. R. Taskinar could not forgive his opponent was that gained in the struggle over the state elections. Notwithstanding his efforts, his threats, and his libels, not to mention the millions of dollars squandered by his electoral courtiers, it was William W. Kolderup who sat in his seat in the Legislative Council of Sacramento.

J. R. Taskinar had learnt—how, I cannot tell—that it was the intention of William W. Kolderup to acquire possession of Spencer Island. This island seemed doubtless as useless to him as it did to his rival. No matter. Here was another chance for fighting, and perhaps for conquering. J. R. Taskinar would not allow it to escape him.

And that is why J. R. Taskinar had come to the auction room among the curious crowd who could not be aware of his designs, why at all points he had prepared his batteries, why before opening fire, he had waited till his opponent had covered the reserve, and why when William W. Kolderup had made his bid of—

"Twelve hundred thousand dollars!"

J. R. Taskinar at the moment when William W. Kolderup thought he had definitely secured the island, woke up with the words shouted in stentorian tones,—

9

"Thirteen hundred thousand dollars!"

Everybody as we have seen turned to look at him.

"Fat Taskinar!"

The name passed from mouth to mouth. Yes. Fat Taskinar! He was known well enough! His corpulence had been the theme of many an article in the journals of the Union.

I am not quite sure which mathematician it was who had demonstrated by transcendental calculations, that so great was his mass that it actually influenced that of our satellite and in an appreciable manner disturbed the elements of the lunar orbit.

But it was not J. R. Taskinar's physical composition which interested the spectators in the room. It was something far different which excited them; it was that he had entered into direct public rivalry with William W. Kolderup. It was a fight of heroes, dollar versus dollar, which had opened, and I do not know which of the two coffers would turn out to be best lined. Enormously rich were both these mortal enemies! After the first sensation, which was rapidly suppressed, renewed silence fell on the assembly. You could have heard a spider weaving his web.

It was the voice of Dean Felporg which broke the spell.

"For thirteen hundred thousand dollars, Spencer Island!" declaimed he, drawing himself up so as to better command the circle of bidders.

William W. Kolderup had turned towards J. R. Taskinar. The bystanders moved back, so as to allow the adversaries to behold each other. The man of Stockton and the man of San Francisco were face to face, mutually staring, at their ease. Truth compels me to state that they made the most of the opportunity. Never would one of them consent to lower his eyes before those of his rival.

"Fourteen hundred thousand dollars," said William W. Kolderup.

"Fifteen hundred thousand!" retorted J. R. Taskinar.

"Sixteen hundred thousand!"

"Seventeen hundred thousand!"

Have you ever heard the story of the two mechanics of Glasgow, who tried which should raise the other highest up the factory chimney at the risk of a catastrophe? The only difference was that here the chimney was of ingots of gold.

Each time after the capping bid of J. R. Taskinar, William W. Kolderup took a few moments to reflect before he bid again. On the contrary Taskinar burst out like a bomb, and did not seem to require a second to think.

"Seventeen hundred thousand dollars!" repeated the

10

auctioneer. "Now, gentlemen, that is a mere nothing! It is giving it away!"

And one can well believe that, carried away by the jargon of his profession, he was about to add,—

"The frame alone is worth more than that!" When—

"Seventeen hundred thousand dollars!" howled Gingrass, the crier.

"Eighteen hundred thousand!" replied William W. Kolderup.

"Nineteen hundred thousand!" retorted J. R. Taskinar.

"Two millions!" quoth William W. Kolderup, and so quickly that this time he evidently had not taken the trouble to think. His face was a little pale when these last words escaped his lips, but his whole attitude was that of a man who did not intend to give in.

J. R. Taskinar was simply on fire. His enormous face was like one of those gigantic railway bull's-eyes which, screened by the red, signal the stoppage of the train. But it was highly probable that his rival would disregard the block, and decline to shut off steam.

This J. R. Taskinar felt. The blood mounted to his brows, and seemed apoplectically congested there. He wriggled his fat fingers, covered with diamonds of great price, along the huge gold chain attached to his chronometer. He glared at his adversary, and then shutting his eyes so as to open them with a more spiteful expression a moment afterwards.

"Two million, four hundred thousand dollars!" he remarked, hoping by this tremendous leap to completely rout his rival.

"Two million, seven hundred thousand!" replied William W. Kolderup in a peculiarly calm voice.

"Two million, nine hundred thousand!"

"Three millions!"

Yes! William W. Kolderup, of San Francisco, said three millions of dollars!

Applause rang through the room, hushed, however, at the voice of the auctioneer, who repeated the bid, and whose oscillating hammer threatened to fall in spite of himself by the involuntary movement of his muscles. It seemed as though Dean Felporg, surfeited with the surprises of public auction sales, would be unable to contain himself any longer.

All glances were turned on J. R. Taskinar. That voluminous personage was sensible of this, but still more was he sensible of the weight of these three millions of dollars, which seemed to crush him. He would have spoken, doubtless to bid higher—but he could not. He would have liked to nod his head—he could do so no more.

11

After a long pause, however, his voice was heard; feeble it is true, but sufficiently audible.

"Three millions, five hundred thousand!"

"Four millions," was the answer of William W. Kolderup.

It was the last blow of the bludgeon. J. R. Taskinar[Pg succumbed. The hammer gave a hard rap on the marble table and—

Spencer Island fell for four millions of dollars to William W. Kolderup, of San Francisco.

"I will be avenged!" muttered J. R. Taskinar, and throwing a glance of hatred at his conqueror, he returned to the Occidental Hotel.

But "hip, hip, hurrah," three times thrice, smote the ears of William W. Kolderup, then cheers followed him to Montgomery Street, and such was the delirious enthusiasm of the Americans that they even forgot to favour him with the customary bars of "Yankee Doodle."

CHAPTER III

THE CONVERSATION OF PHINA HOLLANEY AND GODFREY MORGAN, WITH A PIANO ACCOMPANIMENT

William W. Kolderup had returned to his mansion in Montgomery Street. This thoroughfare is the Regent Street, the Broadway, the Boulevard des Italiens of San Francisco. Throughout its length, the great artery which crosses the city parallel with its quays is astir with life and movement; trams there are innumerable; carriages with horses, carriages with mules; men bent on business, hurrying to and fro over its stone pavements, past shops thronged with customers; men bent on pleasure, crowding the doors of the "bars," where at all hours are dispensed the Californian's drinks.

There is no need for us to describe the mansion of a Frisco nabob. With so many millions, there was proportionate luxury. More comfort than taste. Less of the artistic than the practical. One cannot have everything.

So the reader must be contented to know that there was a magnificent reception-room, and in this reception-room a piano, whose chords were permeating the mansion's warm atmosphere when the opulent Kolderup walked in.

"Good!" he said. "She and he are there! A word to my cashier, and then we can have a little chat."

And he stepped towards his office to arrange the little matter of Spencer Island, and then dismiss it from his mind. He had only to realize a few certificates in his portfolio and the acquisition was settled for. Half-a-dozen lines to his broker—no more. Then William W. Kolderup devoted himself to another "combination" which was much more to his taste.

Yes! she and he were in the drawing-room—she, in front of the piano; he, half reclining on the sofa, listening vaguely to the pearly arpeggios which escaped from the fingers of the charmer.

"Are you listening?" she said.

"Of course."

"Yes! but do you understand it?"

"Do I understand it, Phina! Never have you played those 'Auld Robin Gray' variations more superbly."

"But it is not 'Auld Robin Gray,' Godfrey: it is 'Happy Moments.'"

"Oh! ah! yes! I remember!" answered Godfrey, in a tone of

13

indifference which it was difficult to mistake. The lady raised her two hands, held them suspended for an instant above the keys as if they were about to grasp another chord, and then with a half-turn on her music-stool she remained for a moment looking at the too tranquil Godfrey, whose eyes did their best to avoid hers.

Phina Hollaney was the goddaughter of William W. Kolderup. An orphan, he had educated her, and given her the right to consider herself his daughter, and to love him as her father. She wanted for nothing. She was young, "handsome in her way" as people say, but undoubtedly fascinating, a blonde of sixteen with the ideas of a woman much older, as one could read in the crystal of her blue-black eyes. Of course, we must compare her to a lily, for all beauties are compared to lilies in the best American society. She was then a lily, but a lily grafted into an eglantine. She certainly had plenty of spirit, but she had also plenty of practical common-sense, a somewhat selfish demeanour, and but little sympathy with the illusions and dreams so characteristic of her sex and age.

Her dreams were when she was asleep, not when she was awake. She was not asleep now, and had no intention of being so.

"Godfrey?" she continued.

"Phina?" answered the young man.

"Where are you now?"

"Near you—in this room—"

"Not near me, Godfrey! Not in this room! But far far away, over the seas, is it not so?"

And mechanically Phina's hand sought the key-board and rippled along a series of sinking sevenths, which spoke of a plaintive sadness, unintelligible perhaps to the nephew of William W. Kolderup.

For such was this young man, such was the relationship he bore towards the master of the house. The son of a sister of this buyer of islands, fatherless and motherless for a good many years, Godfrey Morgan, like Phina, had been brought up in the house of his uncle, in whom the fever of business had still left a place for the idea of marrying these two to each other.

Godfrey was in his twenty-third year. His education now finished, had left him with absolutely nothing to do. He had graduated at the University, but had found it of little use. For him life opened out but paths of ease; go where he would, to the right or the left, whichever way he went, fortune would not fail him.

Godfrey was of good presence, gentlemanly, elegant—never tying his cravat in a ring, nor starring his fingers, his wrists or his

14

shirt-front with those jewelled gimcracks so dear to his fellow-citizens.

I shall surprise no one in saying that Godfrey Morgan was going to marry Phina Hollaney. Was he likely to do otherwise? All the proprieties were in favour of it. Besides, William W. Kolderup desired the marriage. The two people whom he loved most in this world were sure of a fortune from him, without taking into consideration whether Phina cared for Godfrey, or Godfrey cared for Phina. It would also simplify the bookkeeping of the commercial house. Ever since their births an account had been opened for the boy, another for the girl. It would then be only necessary to rule these off and transfer the balances to a joint account for the young couple. The worthy merchant hoped that this would soon be done, and the balances struck without error or omission.

But it is precisely that there had been an omission and perhaps an error that we are about to show.

An error, because at the outset Godfrey felt that he was not yet old enough for the serious undertaking of marriage; an omission, because he had not been consulted on the subject.

In fact, when he had finished his studies Godfrey had displayed a quite premature indifference to the world, in which he wanted for nothing, in which he had no wish remaining ungratified, and nothing whatever to do. The thought of travelling round the world was always present to him. Of the old and new continents he knew but one spot—San Francisco, where he was born, and which he had never left except in a dream. What harm was there in a young man making the tour of the globe twice or thrice—especially if he were an American? Would it do him any good? Would he learn anything in the different adventures he would meet with in a voyage of any length? If he were not already satiated with a life of adventure, how could he be answered? Finally, how many millions of leagues of observation and instruction were indispensable for the completion of the young man's education?

Things had reached this pass; for a year or more Godfrey had been immersed in books of voyages of recent date, and had passionately devoured them. He had discovered the Celestial Empire with Marco Polo, America with Columbus, the Pacific with Cook, the South Pole with Dumont d'Urville. He had conceived the idea of going where these illustrious travellers had been without him. In truth, he would not have considered an exploring expedition of several years to cost him too dear at the price of a few attacks of Malay pirates, several ocean collisions, and a shipwreck or two on a desert island where he could live the life of a Selkirk or a Robinson

15

Crusoe! A Crusoe! To become a Crusoe! What young imagination has not dreamt of this in reading as Godfrey had often, too often done, the adventures of the imaginary heroes of Daniel de Foe and De Wyss?

Yes! The nephew of William W. Kolderup was in this state when his uncle was thinking of binding him in the chains of marriage. To travel in this way with Phina, then become Mrs. Morgan, would be clearly impossible! He must go alone or leave it alone. Besides, once his fancy had passed away, would not she be better disposed to sign the settlements? Was it for the good of his wife that he had not been to China or Japan, not even to Europe? Decidedly not.

And hence it was that Godfrey was now absent in the presence of Phina, indifferent when she spoke to him, deaf when she played the airs which used to please him; and Phina, like a thoughtful, serious girl, soon noticed this.

To say that she did not feel a little annoyance mingled with some chagrin, is to do her a gratuitous injustice. But accustomed to look things in the face, she had reasoned thus,—

"If we must part, it had better be before marriage than afterwards!"

And thus it was that she had spoken to Godfrey in these significant words.

"No! You are not near me at this moment—you are beyond the seas!"

Godfrey had risen. He had walked a few steps without noticing Phina, and unconsciously his index finger touched one of the keys of the piano. A loud C# of the octave below the staff, a note dismal enough, answered for him.

Phina had understood him, and without more discussion was about to bring matters to a crisis, when the door of the room opened.

William W. Kolderup appeared, seemingly a little preoccupied as usual. Here was the merchant who had just finished one negotiation and was about to begin another.

"Well," said he, "there is nothing more now than for us to fix the date."

"The date?" answered Godfrey, with a start. "What date, if you please, uncle?"

"The date of your wedding!" said William W. Kolderup. "Not the date of mine, I suppose!"

"Perhaps that is more urgent?" said Phina.

16

"Hey?—what?" exclaimed the uncle—"what does that matter? We are only talking of current affairs, are we not?"

"Godfather Will," answered the lady. "It is not of a wedding that we are going to fix the date to-day, but of a departure."

"A departure!"

"Yes, the departure of Godfrey," continued Phina, "of Godfrey who, before he gets married, wants to see a little of the world!"

"You want to go away—you?" said William W. Kolderup, stepping towards the young man and raising his arms as if he were afraid that this "rascal of a nephew" would escape him.

"Yes; I do, uncle," said Godfrey gallantly.

"And for how long?"

"For eighteen months, or two years, or more, if—"

"If—"

"If you will let me, and Phina will wait for me."

"Wait for you! An intended who intends until he gets away!" exclaimed William W. Kolderup.

"You must let Godfrey go," pleaded Phina; "I have thought it carefully over. I am young, but really Godfrey is younger. Travel will age him, and I do not think it will change his taste! He wishes to travel, let him travel! The need of repose will come to him afterwards, and he will find me when he returns."

"What!" exclaimed William W. Kolderup, "you consent to give your bird his liberty?"

"Yes, for the two years he asks."

"And you will wait for him?"

"Uncle Will, if I could not wait for him I could not love him!" and so saying Phina returned to the piano, and whether she willed it or no, her fingers softly played a portion of the then fashionable "Départ du Fiancé," which was very appropriate under the circumstances. But Phina, without perceiving it perhaps, was playing in "A minor," whereas it was written in "A major," and all the sentiment of the melody was transformed, and its plaintiveness chimed in well with her hidden feelings.

But Godfrey stood embarrassed, and said not a word. His uncle took him by the head and turning it to the light looked fixedly at him for a moment or two. In this way he questioned him without having to speak, and Godfrey was able to reply without having occasion to utter a syllable.

And the lamentations of the "Départ du Fiancé" continued their sorrowful theme, and then William W. Kolderup, having made the turn of the room, returned to Godfrey, who stood like a criminal before the judge. Then raising his voice,—

"You are serious," he asked.

"Quite serious!" interrupted Phina, while Godfrey contented himself with making a sign of affirmation.

"You want to try travelling before you marry Phina! Well! You shall try it, my nephew!"

He made two or three steps and stopping with crossed arms before Godfrey, asked,—

"Where do you want to go to?"

"Everywhere."

"And when do you want to start?"

"When you please, Uncle Will."

"All right," replied William W. Kolderup, fixing a curious look on his nephew.

Then he muttered between his teeth,—

"The sooner the better."

At these last words came a sudden interruption from Phina. The little finger of her left hand touched a G#, and the fourth had, instead of falling on the key-note, rested on the "sensible," like Ralph in the "Huguenots," when he leaves at the end of his duet with Valentine.

Perhaps Phina's heart was nearly full, she had made up her mind to say nothing.

It was then that William W. Kolderup, without noticing Godfrey, approached the piano.

"Phina," said he gravely, "you should never remain on the 'sensible'!"

And with the tip of his large finger he dropped vertically on to one of the keys and an "A natural" resounded through the room.

CHAPTER IV

IN WHICH T. ARTELETT, OTHERWISE TARTLET, IS DULY INTRODUCED TO THE READER

If T. Artelett had been a Parisian, his compatriots would not have failed to nickname him Tartlet, but as he had already received this title we do not hesitate to describe him by it. If Tartlet was not a Frenchman he ought to have been one.

In his "Itinéraire de Paris à Jérusalem," Chateaubriand tells of a little man "powdered and frizzed in the old-fashioned style, with a coat of apple green, a waistcoat of drouget, shirt-frill and cuffs of muslin, who scraped a violin and made the Iroquois dance 'Madeleine Friquet.'"

The Californians are not Iroquois, far from it; but Tartlet was none the less professor of dancing and deportment in the capital of their state. If they did not pay him for his lessons, as they had his predecessor in beaver-skins and bear-hams, they did so in dollars. If in speaking of his pupils he did not talk of the "bucks and their squaws," it was because his pupils were highly civilized, and because in his opinion he had contributed considerably to their civilization.

Tartlet was a bachelor, and aged about forty-five at the time we introduce him to our readers. But for a dozen years or so his marriage with a lady of somewhat mature age had been expected to take place.

Under present circumstances it is perhaps advisable to give "two or three lines" concerning his age, appearance, and position in life. He would have responded to such a request we imagine as follows, and thus we can dispense with drawing his portrait from a moral and physical point of view.

"He was born on the 17th July, 1835, at a quarter-past three in the morning.

"His height is five feet, two inches, three lines.

"His girth is exactly two feet, three inches.

"His weight, increased by some six pounds during the last year, is one hundred and fifty one pounds, two ounces.

"He has an oblong head.

"His hair, very thin above the forehead, is grey chestnut, his forehead is high, his face oval, his complexion fresh coloured.

"His eyes—sight excellent—a greyish brown, eyelashes and

eyebrows clear chestnut, eyes themselves somewhat sunk in their orbits beneath the arches of the brows.

"His nose is of medium size, and has a slight indentation towards the end of the left nostril.

"His cheeks and temples are flat and hairless.

"His ears are large and flat.

"His mouth, of middling size, is absolutely free from bad teeth.

"His lips, thin and slightly pinched, are covered with a heavy moustache and imperial, his chin is round and also shaded with a many-tinted beard.

"A small mole ornaments his plump neck—in the nape.

"Finally, when he is in the bath it can be seen that his skin is white and smooth.

"His life is calm and regular. Without being robust, thanks to his great temperance, he has kept his health uninjured since his birth. His lungs are rather irritable, and hence he has not contracted the bad habit of smoking. He drinks neither spirits, coffee, liqueurs, nor neat wine. In a word, all that could prejudicially affect his nervous system is vigorously excluded from his table. Light beer, and weak wine and water are the only beverages he can take without danger. It is on account of his carefulness that he has never had to consult a doctor since his life began.

"His gesture is prompt, his walk quick, his character frank and open. His thoughtfulness for others is extreme, and it is on account of this that in the fear of making his wife unhappy, he has never entered into matrimony."

Such would have been the report furnished by Tartlet, but desirable as he might be to a lady of a certain age, the projected union had hitherto failed. The professor remained a bachelor, and continued to give lessons in dancing and deportment.

It was in this capacity that he entered the mansion of William W. Kolderup. As time rolled on his pupils gradually abandoned him, and he ended by becoming one wheel more in the machinery of the wealthy establishment.

After all, he was a brave man, in spite of his eccentricities. Everybody liked him. He liked Godfrey, he liked Phina, and they liked him. He had only one ambition in the world, and that was to teach them all the secrets of his art, to make them in fact, as far as deportment was concerned, two highly accomplished individuals.

Now, what would you think? It was he, this Professor Tartlet, whom William W. Kolderup had chosen as his nephew's companion during the projected voyage. Yes! He had reason to believe that

Tartlet had not a little contributed to imbue Godfrey with this roaming mania, so as to perfect himself by a tour round the world. William W. Kolderup had resolved that they should go together. On the morrow, the 16th of April, he sent for the professor to his office.

The request of the nabob was an order for Tartlet. The professor left his room, with his pocket violin—generally known as a kit—so as to be ready for all emergencies. He mounted the great staircase of the mansion with his feet academically placed as was fitting for a dancing-master; knocked at the door of the room, entered—his body half inclined, his elbows rounded, his mouth on the grin—and waited in the third position, after having crossed his feet one before the other, at half their length, his ankles touching and his toes turned out. Any one but Professor Tartlet placed in this sort of unstable equilibrium would have tottered on his base, but the professor preserved an absolute perpendicularity.

"Mr. Tartlet," said William W. Kolderup, "I have sent for you to tell you some news which I imagine will rather surprise you."

"As you think best!" answered the professor.

"My nephew's marriage is put off for a year or eighteen months, and Godfrey, at his own request, is going to visit the different countries of the old and new world."

"Sir," answered Tartlet, "my pupil, Godfrey, will do honour to the country of his birth, and—"

"And, to the professor of deportment who has initiated him into etiquette," interrupted the merchant, in a tone of which the guileless Tartlet failed to perceive the irony.

And, in fact, thinking it the correct thing to execute an "assemblée," he first moved one foot and then the other, by a sort of semi-circular side slide, and then with a light and graceful bend of the knee, he bowed to William W. Kolderup.

"I thought," continued the latter, "that you might feel a little regret at separating from your pupil?"

"The regret will be extreme," answered Tartlet, "but should it be necessary—"

"It is not necessary," answered William W. Kolderup, knitting his bushy eyebrows.

"Ah!" replied Tartlet.

Slightly troubled, he made a graceful movement to the rear, so as to pass from the third to the fourth position; but he left the breadth of a foot between his feet, without perhaps being conscious of what he was doing.

"Yes!" added the merchant in a peremptory tone, which

21

admitted not of the ghost of a reply; "I have thought it would really be cruel to separate a professor and a pupil so well made to understand each other!"

"Assuredly!—the journey?" answered Tartlet, who did not seem to want to understand.

"Yes! Assuredly!" replied William W. Kolderup; "not only will his travels bring out the talents of my nephew, but the talents of the professor to whom he owes so correct a bearing."

Never had the thought occurred to this great baby that one day he would leave San Francisco, California, America, to roam the seas. Such an idea had never entered the brain of a man more absorbed in choregraphy than geography, and who was still ignorant of the suburbs of the capital beyond ten miles radius. And now this was offered to him. He was to understand that *nolens volens* he was to expatriate himself, he himself was to experience with all their costs and inconveniences the very adventures he had recommended to his pupil! Here, decidedly, was something to trouble a brain much more solid than his, and the unfortunate Tartlet for the first time in his life felt an involuntary yielding in the muscles of his limbs, suppled as they were by thirty-five years' exercise.

"Perhaps," said he, trying to recall to his lips the stereotyped smile of the dancer which had left him for an instant,—"perhaps— am I not—"

"You will go!" answered William W. Kolderup like a a man with whom discussion was useless.

To refuse was impossible. Tartlet did not even think of such a thing. What was he in the house? A thing, a parcel, a package to be sent to every corner of the world. But the projected expedition troubled him not a little.

"And when am I to start?" demanded he, trying to get back into an academical position.

"In a month."

"And on what raging ocean has Mr. Kolderup decided that his vessel should bear his nephew and me?"

"The Pacific, at first."

"And on what point of the terrestrial globe shall I first set foot?"

"On the soil of New Zealand," answered William W. Kolderup; "I have remarked that the New Zealanders always stick their elbows out! Now you can teach them to turn them in!"

And thus was Professor Tartlet selected as the travelling-companion of Godfrey Morgan.

A nod from the merchant gave him to understand that the audience had terminated. He retired, considerably agitated, and the performance of the special graces which he usually displayed in this difficult act left a good deal to be desired. In fact, for the first time in his life, Professor Tartlet, forgetting in his preoccupation the most elementary principles of his art, went out with his toes turned in!

CHAPTER V

IN WHICH THEY PREPARE TO GO, AND AT THE END OF WHICH THEY GO FOR GOOD

Before the long voyage together through life, which men call marriage, Godfrey then was to make the tour of the world—a journey sometimes even more dangerous. But he reckoned on returning improved in every respect; he left a lad, he would return a man. He would have seen, noted, compared. His curiosity would be satisfied. There would only remain for him to settle down quietly, and live happily at home with his wife, whom no temptation would take him from. Was he wrong or right? Was he to learn a valuable lesson? The future will show.

In short, Godfrey was enchanted.

Phina, anxious without appearing to be so, was resigned to this apprenticeship.

Professor Tartlet, generally so firm on his limbs, had lost all his dancing equilibrium. He had lost all his usual self-possession, and tried in vain to recover it; he even tottered on the carpet of his room as if he were already on the floor of a cabin, rolling and pitching on the ocean.

As for William W. Kolderup, since he had arrived at a decision, he had become very uncommunicative, especially to his nephew. The closed lips, and eyes half hidden beneath their lids, showed that there was some fixed idea in the head where generally floated the highest commercial speculations.

"Ah! you want to travel," muttered he every now and then; "travel instead of marrying and staying at home! Well, you shall travel."

Preparations were immediately begun.

In the first place, the itinerary had to be projected, discussed, and settled.

Was Godfrey to go south, or east, or west? That had to be decided in the first place.

If he went southwards, the Panama, California and British Columbia Company, or the Southampton and Rio Janeiro Company would have to take him to Europe.

If he went eastwards, the Union Pacific Railway would take him in a few days to New York, and thence the Cunard, Inman,

White Star, Hamburg-American, or French-Transatlantic Companies would land him on the shores of the old world.

If he went westwards, the Golden Age Steam Transoceanic would render it easy for him to reach Melbourne, and thence he could get to the Isthmus of Suez by the boats of the Peninsular and Oriental Company.

The means of transport were abundant, and thanks to their mathematical agreement the round of the world was but a simple pleasure tour.

But it was not thus that the nephew and heir of the nabob of Frisco was to travel.

No! William W. Kolderup possessed for the requirements of his business quite a fleet of steam and sailing-vessels. He had decided that one of these ships should be "put at the disposal" of Godfrey Morgan, as if he were a prince of the blood, travelling for his pleasure—at the expense of his father's subjects.

By his orders the *Dream*, a substantial steamer of 600 tons and 200 horse-power, was got ready. It was to be commanded by Captain Turcott, a tough old salt, who had already sailed in every latitude in every sea. A thorough sailor, this friend of tornadoes, cyclones, and typhoons, had already spent of his fifty years of life, forty at sea. To bring to in a hurricane was quite child's play to this mariner, who was never disconcerted, except by land-sickness when he was in port. His incessantly unsteady existence on a vessel's deck had endowed him with the habit of constantly balancing himself to the right or the left, or behind or in front, as though he had the rolling and pitching variety of St. Vitus's dance.

A mate, an engineer, four stokers, a dozen seamen, eighteen men in all, formed the crew of the *Dream*. And if the ship was contented to get quietly through eight miles an hour, she possessed a great many excellent nautical qualities. If she was not swift enough to race the waves when the sea was high, the waves could not race over her, and that was an advantage which quite compensated for the mediocrity of her speed, particularly when there was no hurry. The *Dream* was brigantine rigged, and in a favourable wind, with her 400 square yards of canvas, her steaming rate could be considerably increased.

It should be borne in mind all through that the voyage of the *Dream* was carefully planned, and would be punctually performed. William W. Kolderup was too practical a man not to put to some purpose a journey of 15,000 or 16,000 leagues across all the oceans of the globe. His ship was to go without cargo, undoubtedly, but it was easy to get her down to her right trim by means of water ballast, and even to sink her to her deck, if it proved necessary.

The *Dream* was instructed to communicate with the different branch establishments of the wealthy merchant. She was to go from one market to another.

Captain Turcott, never fear, would not find it difficult to pay the expenses of the voyage! Godfrey Morgan's whim would not cost the avuncular purse a single dollar! That is the way they do business in the best commercial houses!

All this was decided at long, very secret interviews between William W. Kolderup and Captain Turcott. But it appeared that the regulation of this matter, simple as it seemed, could not be managed alone, for the captain paid numerous visits to the merchant's office. When he came away, it would be noticed that his face bore a curious expression, that his hair stood on end as if he had been ruffling it up with fevered hands, and that all his body rolled and pitched more than usual. High words were constantly heard, proving that the interviews were stormy. Captain Turcott, with his plain speaking, knew how to withstand William W. Kolderup, who loved and esteemed him enough to permit him to contradict him.

And now all was arranged. Who had given in? William W. Kolderup or Turcott? I dare not say, for I do not even know the subject of their discussion. However, I rather think it must have been the captain.

Anyhow, after eight days of interviewing, the merchant and the captain were in accord, but Turcott did not cease to grumble between his teeth.

"May five hundred thousand Davy Joneses drag me to the bottom if ever I had a job like this before!"

However, the *Dream* fitted out rapidly, and her captain neglected nothing which would enable him to put to sea in the first fortnight in June. She had been into dock, and the hull had been gone over with composition, whose brilliant red contrasted vividly with the black of her upper works.

A great number of vessels of all kinds and nationalities came into the port of San Francisco. In a good many years the old quays of the town, built straight along the shore, would have been insufficient for the embarkation and disembarkation of their cargoes, if engineers had not devised subsidiary wharves. Piles of red deal were driven into the water, and many square miles of planks were laid on them and formed huge platforms. A good deal of the bay was thus taken up, but the bay is enormous. There were also regular landing-stages, with numberless cranes and crabs, at

26

which steamers from both oceans, steamboats from the Californian rivers, clippers from all countries, and coasters from the American seaboard were ranged in proper order, so as not to interfere one with the other.

It was at one of these artificial quays, at the extremity of Mission Wharf Street, that the *Dream* had been securely moored after she had come out of dock.

Nothing was neglected, and the steamer would start under the most favourable conditions. Provisioning, outfit, all were minutely studied. The rigging was perfect, the boilers had been tested and the screw was an excellent one. A steam launch was even carried, to facilitate communication with the shore, and this would probably be of great service during the voyage.

Everything was ready on the 10th of June. They had only to put to sea. The men shipped by Captain Turcott to work the sails or drive the engine were a picked crew, and it would have been difficult to find a better one. Quite a stock of live animals, agouties, sheep, goats, poultry, &c., were stowed between decks, the material wants of the travellers were likewise provided for by numerous cases of preserved meats of the best brands.

The route the *Dream* was to follow had doubtless been the subject of the long conferences which William W. Kolderup had had with his captain. All knew that they were first bound for Auckland, in New Zealand, unless want of coal necessitated by the persistence of contrary winds obliged them to refill perhaps at one of the islands of the Pacific or some Chinese port.

All this detail mattered little to Godfrey once he was on the sea, and still less to Tartlet, whose troubled spirit exaggerated from day to day the dangers of navigation. There was only one formality to be gone through—the formality of being photographed.

An engaged man could not decently start on a long voyage round the world without taking with him the image of her he loved, and in return leaving his own image behind him.

Godfrey in tourist costume accordingly handed himself over to Messrs Stephenson and Co., photographers of Montgomery Street, and Phina, in her walking-dress, confided in like manner to the sun the task of fixing her charming but somewhat sorrowing features on the plate of those able operators.

It is also the custom to travel together, and so Phina's portrait had its allotted place in Godfrey's cabin, and Godfrey's portrait its special position in Phina's room. As for Tartlet, who had no betrothed and who was not thinking of having one at present, he thought it better to confide his image to sensitised paper. But

27

although great was the talent of the photographers they failed to present him with a satisfactory proof. The negative was a confused fog in which it was impossible to recognize the celebrated professor of dancing and deportment.

This was because the patient could not keep himself still, in spite of all that was said about the invariable rule in studios devoted to operations of this nature.

They tried other means, even the instantaneous process. Impossible. Tartlet pitched and rolled in anticipation as violently as the captain of the *Dream*.

The idea of obtaining a picture of the features of this remarkable man had thus to be abandoned. Irreparable would be the misfortune if—but far from us be the thought!—if in imagining he was leaving the new world for the old world Tartlet had left the new world for the other world from which nobody returns.

On the 9th of June all was ready. The *Dream* was complete. Her papers, bills of lading, charter-party, assurance policy, were all in order, and two days before the ship-broker had sent on the last signatures.

On that day a grand farewell breakfast was given at the mansion in Montgomery Street. They drank to the happy voyage of Godfrey and his safe return.

Godfrey was rather agitated, and he did not strive to hide it. Phina showed herself much the most composed. As for Tartlet he drowned his apprehensions in several glasses of champagne, whose influence was perceptible up to the moment of departure. He even forgot his kit, which was brought to him as they were casting off the last hawsers of the *Dream*.

The last adieux were said on board, the last handshakings took place on the poop, then the engine gave two or three turns of the screw and the steamer was under way.

"Good-bye, Phina!"

"Good-bye, Godfrey!"

"May Heaven protect you!" said the uncle.

"And above all may it bring us back!" murmured Professor Tartlet.

"And never forget, Godfrey," added William W. Kolderup, "the device which the *Dream* bears on her stern, 'Confide, recte agens.'"

"Never, Uncle Will! Good-bye, Phina!"

"Good-bye, Godfrey!"

The steamer moved off, handkerchiefs were shaken as long as she remained in sight from the quay, and even after. Soon the bay of San Francisco, the largest in the world, was crossed, the *Dream* passed the narrow throat of the Golden Gate and then her prow cleft the waters of the Pacific Ocean. It was as though the Gates of Gold had closed upon her.

CHAPTER VI

IN WHICH THE READER MAKES THE ACQUAINTANCE OF A NEW PERSONAGE

The voyage had begun. There had not been much difficulty so far, it must be admitted.

Professor Tartlet, with incontestable logic, often repeated,—

"Any voyage can begin! But where and how it finishes is the important point."

The cabin occupied by Godfrey was below the poop of the *Dream* and opened on to the dining-saloon. Our young traveller was lodged there as comfortably as possible. He had given Phina's photograph the best place on the best lighted panel of his room. A cot to sleep on, a lavatory for toilet purposes, some chests of drawers for his clothes and his linen, a table to work at, an armchair to sit upon, what could a young man in his twenty-second year want more? Under such circumstances he might have gone twenty-two times round the world! Was he not at the age of that practical philosophy which consists in good health and good humour? Ah! young people, travel if you can, and if you cannot—travel all the same!

Tartlet was not in a good humour. His cabin, near that of his pupil, seemed to him too narrow, his bed too hard, the six square yards which he occupied quite insufficient for his steps and strides. Would not the traveller in him absorb the professor of dancing and deportment? No! It was in the blood, and when Tartlet reached the hour of his last sleep his feet would be found placed in a horizontal line with the heels one against the other, in the first position.

Meals were taken in common. Godfrey and Tartlet sat opposite to each other, the captain and mate occupying each end of the rolling table. This alarming appellation, the "rolling table," is enough to warn us that the professor's place would too often be vacant.

At the start, in the lovely month of June, there was a beautiful breeze from the north-east, and Captain Turcott was able to set his canvas so as to increase his speed. The *Dream* thus balanced hardly rolled at all, and as the waves followed her, her pitching was but slight. This mode of progressing was not such as to affect the looks of the passengers and give them pinched noses, hollow eyes, livid foreheads, or colourless cheeks. It was supportable. They steered south-west over a splendid sea, hardly lifting in the least, and the American coast soon disappeared below the horizon.

For two days nothing occurred worthy of mention. The *Dream* made good progress. The commencement of the voyage promised well—so that Captain Turcott seemed occasionally to feel an anxiety which he tried in vain to hide. Each day as the sun crossed the meridian he carefully took his observations. But it could be noticed that immediately afterwards he retired with the mate into his cabin, and then they remained in secret conclave as if they were discussing some grave eventuality. This performance passed probably unnoticed by Godfrey, who understood nothing about the details of navigation, but the boatswain and the crew seemed somewhat astonished at it, particularly as for two or three times during the first week, when there was not the least necessity for the manœuvre, the course of the *Dream* at night was completely altered, and resumed again in the morning. In a sailing-ship this might be intelligible; but in a steamer, which could keep on the great circle line and only use canvas when the wind was favourable, it was somewhat extraordinary.

During the morning of the 12th of June a very unexpected incident occurred on board.

Captain Turcott, the mate, and Godfrey, were sitting down to breakfast when an unusual noise was heard on deck. Almost immediately afterwards the boatswain opened the door and appeared on the threshold.

"Captain!" he said.

"What's up?" asked Turcott, sailor as he was, always on the alert.

"Here's a—Chinee!" said the boatswain.

"A Chinese!"

"Yes! a genuine Chinese we have just found by chance at the bottom of the hold!"

"At the bottom of the hold!" exclaimed Turcott. "Well, by all the—somethings—of Sacramento, just send him to the bottom of the sea!"

"All right!" answered the boatswain.

And that excellent man with all the contempt of a Californian for a son of the Celestial Empire, taking the order as quite a natural one, would have had not the slightest compunction in executing it.

However, Captain Turcott rose from his chair, and followed by Godfrey and the mate, left the saloon and walked towards the forecastle of the *Dream*.

There stood a Chinaman, tightly handcuffed, and held by two

31

or three sailors, who were by no means sparing of their nudges and knocks. He was a man of from five-and-thirty to forty, with intelligent features, well built, of lithe figure, but a little emaciated, owing to his sojourn for sixteen hours at the bottom of a badly ventilated hold.

Captain Turcott made a sign to his men to leave the unhappy intruder alone.

"Who are you?" he asked.

"A son of the sun."

"And what is your name?"

"Seng Vou," answered the Chinese, whose name in the Celestial language signifies "he who does not live."

"And what are you doing on board here?"

"I am out for a sail!" coolly answered Seng Vou, "but am doing you as little harm as I can."

"Really! as little harm!—and you stowed yourself away in the hold when we started?"

"Just so, captain."

"So that we might take you for nothing from America to China, on the other side of the Pacific?"

"If you will have it so."

"And if I don't wish to have it so, you yellow-skinned nigger. If I will have it that you have to swim to China."

"I will try," said the Chinaman with a smile, "but I shall probably sink on the road!"

"Well, John," exclaimed Captain Turcott, "I am going to show you how to save your passage-money."

And Captain Turcott, much more angry than circumstances necessitated, was perhaps about to put his threat into execution, when Godfrey intervened.

"Captain," he said, "one more Chinee on board the *Dream* is one Chinee less in California, where there are too many."

"A great deal too many!" answered Captain Turcott.

"Yes, too many. Well, if this poor beggar wishes to relieve San Francisco of his presence, he ought to be pitied! Bah! we can throw him on shore at Shanghai, and there needn't be any fuss about it!"

In saying that there were too many Chinese in California Godfrey held the same language as every true Californian. The emigration of the sons of the Celestial Empire—there are 300,000,000 in China as against 30,000,000 of Americans in the United States—has become dangerous to the provinces of the Far West; and the legislators of these States of California, Lower California, Oregon, Nevada, Utah, and even Congress itself, are much concerned at this new epidemic of invasion, to which the Yankees have given the name of the "yellow-plague."

At this period there were more than 50,000 Chinese, in the State of California alone. These people, very industrious at gold-washing, very patient, living on a pinch of rice, a mouthful of tea, and a whiff of opium, did an immense deal to bring down the price of manual labour, to the detriment of the native workmen. They had to submit to special laws, contrary to the American constitution—laws which regulated their immigration, and withheld from them the right of naturalization, owing to the fear that they would end by obtaining a majority in the Congress. Generally ill-treated, much as Indians or negroes, so as to justify the title of "pests" which was applied to them, they herded together in a sort of ghetto, where they carefully kept up the manners and customs of the Celestial Empire.

In the Californian capital, it is in the Sacramento Street district, decked with their banners and lanterns, that this foreign race has taken up its abode. There they can be met in thousands, trotting along in their wide-sleeved blouses, conical hats, and turned-up shoes. Here, for the most part, they live as grocers, gardeners, or laundresses—unless they are working as cooks or belong to one of those dramatic troupes which perform Chinese pieces in the French theatre at San Francisco.

And—there is no reason why we should conceal the fact—Seng Vou happened to form part of one of these troupes, in which he filled the rôle of "comic lead," if such a description can apply to any Chinese artiste. As a matter of fact they are so serious, even in their fun, that the Californian romancer, Bret Harte, has told us that he never saw a genuine Chinaman laugh, and has even confessed that he is unable to say whether one of the national pieces he witnessed was a tragedy or a farce.

In short, Seng Vou was a comedian. The season had ended, crowned with success—perhaps out of proportion to the gold pieces he had amassed—he wished to return to his country otherwise than as a corpse, for Chinamen always like to get buried at home and there are special steamers who carry dead Celestials and nothing else. At all risks, therefore, he had secretly slipped on board the *Dream*.

Loaded with provisions, did he hope to get through, incognito, a passage of several weeks, and then to land on the coast of China without being seen?

It is just possible. At any rate, the case was hardly one for a death penalty.

So Godfrey had good reason to interfere in favour of the

intruder, and Captain Turcott, who pretended to be angrier than he really was, gave up the idea of sending Seng Vou overboard to battle with the waves of the Pacific.

Seng Vou, however, did not return to his hiding-place in the hold, though he was rather an incubus on board. Phlegmatic, methodic, and by no means communicative, he carefully avoided the seamen, who had always some prank to play off on him, and he kept to his own provisions. He was thin enough in all conscience, and his additional weight but imperceptibly added to the cost of navigating the *Dream*. If Seng Vou got a free passage it was obvious that his carriage did not cost William W. Kolderup very much.

His presence on board put into Captain Turcott's head an idea which his mate probably was the only one to understand thoroughly.

"He will bother us a bit—this confounded Chinee!—after all, so much the worse for him."

"What ever made him stow himself away on board the *Dream*?" answered the mate.

"To get to Shanghai!" replied Captain Turcott. "Bless John and all John's sons too!"

CHAPTER VII

IN WHICH IT WILL BE SEEN THAT WILLIAM W. KOLDERUP WAS PROBABLY RIGHT IN INSURING HIS SHIP

During the following days, the 13th, 14th, and 15th of June, the barometer slowly fell, without an attempt to rise in the slightest degree, and the weather became variable, hovering between rain and wind or storm. The breeze strengthened considerably, and changed to south-westerly. It was a head-wind for the *Dream*, and the waves had now increased enormously, and lifted her forward. The sails were all furled, and she had to depend on her screw alone; under half steam, however, so as to avoid excessive labouring.

Godfrey bore the trial of the ship's motion without even losing his good-humour for a moment. Evidently he was fond of the sea.

But Tartlet was not fond of the sea, and it served him out.

It was pitiful to see the unfortunate professor of deportment deporting himself no longer, the professor of dancing dancing contrary to every rule of his art. Remain in his cabin, with the seas shaking the ship from stem to stern, he could not.

"Air! air!" he gasped.

And so he never left the deck. A roll sent him rolling from one side to the other, a pitch sent him pitching from one end to the other. He clung to the rails, he clutched the ropes, he assumed every attitude that is absolutely condemned by the principles of the modern choregraphic art. Ah! why could he not raise himself into the air by some balloon-like movement, and escape the eccentricities of that moving plane? A dancer of his ancestors had said that he only consented to set foot to the ground so as not to humiliate his companions, but Tartlet would willingly never have come down at all on the deck, whose perpetual agitation threatened to hurl him into the abyss.

What an idea it was for the rich William W. Kolderup to send him here.

"Is this bad weather likely to last?" asked he of Captain Turcott twenty times a day.

"Dunno! barometer is not very promising!" was the invariable answer of the captain, knitting his brows.

"Shall we soon get there?"

"Soon, Mr. Tartlet? Hum! soon!"

35

"And they call this the Pacific Ocean!" repeated the unfortunate man, between a couple of shocks and oscillations.

It should be stated that, not only did Professor Tartlet suffer from sea-sickness, but also that fear had seized him as he watched the great seething waves breaking into foam level with the bulwarks of the *Dream*, and heard the valves, lifted by the violent beats, letting the steam off through the waste-pipes, as he felt the steamer tossing like a cork on the mountains of water.

"No," said he with a lifeless look at his pupil, "it is not impossible for us to capsize."

"Take it quietly, Tartlet," replied Godfrey. "A ship was made to float! There are reasons for all this."

"I tell you there are none."

And, thinking thus, the professor had put on his life-belt. He wore it night and day, tightly buckled round his waist. He would not have taken it off for untold gold. Every time the sea gave him a moment's respite he would replenish it with another puff. In fact, he never blew it out enough to please him.

We must make some indulgence for the terrors of Tartlet. To those unaccustomed to the sea, its rolling is of a nature to cause some alarm, and we know that this passenger-in-spite-of-himself had not even till then risked his safety on the peaceable waters of the Bay of San Francisco; so that we can forgive his being ill on board a ship in a stiffish breeze, and his feeling terrified at the playfulness of the waves.

The weather became worse and worse, and threatened the *Dream* with a gale, which, had she been near the shore, would have been announced to her by the semaphores.

During the day the ship was dreadfully knocked about, though running at half steam so as not to damage her engines. Her screw was continually immerging and emerging in the violent oscillations of her liquid bed. Hence, powerful strokes from its wings in the deeper water, or fearful tremors as it rose and ran wild, causing heavy thunderings beneath the stern, and furious gallopings of the pistons which the engineer could master but with difficulty.

One observation Godfrey made, of which at first he could not discover the cause. This was, that during the night the shocks experienced by the steamer were infinitely less violent than during the day. Was he then to conclude that the wind then fell, and that a calm set in after sundown?

This was so remarkable that, on the night between the 21st and 22nd of June, he endeavoured to find out some explanation of it. The day had been particularly stormy, the wind had freshened, and it did not appear at all likely that the sea would fall at night, lashed so capriciously as it had been for so many hours.

Towards midnight then Godfrey dressed, and, wrapping himself up warmly, went on deck.

The men on watch were forward, Captain Turcott was on the bridge.

The force of the wind had certainly not diminished. The shock of the waves, which should have dashed on the bows of the *Dream*, was, however, very much less violent. But in raising his eyes towards the top of the funnel, with its black canopy of smoke, Godfrey saw that the smoke, instead of floating from the bow aft, was, on the contrary, floating from aft forwards, and following the same direction as the ship.

"Has the wind changed?" he said to himself.

And extremely glad at the circumstance he mounted the bridge. Stepping up to Turcott,—

"Captain!" he said.

The latter, enveloped in his oilskins, had not heard him approach, and at first could not conceal a movement of annoyance in seeing him close to him.

"You, Mr. Godfrey, you—on the bridge?"

"Yes, I, captain. I came to ask—"

"What?" answered Captain Turcott sharply.

"If the wind has not changed?"

"No, Mr. Godfrey, no. And, unfortunately, I think it will turn to a storm!"

"But we now have the wind behind us!"

"Wind behind us—yes—wind behind us!" replied the captain, visibly disconcerted at the observation. "But it is not my fault."

"What do you mean?"

"I mean that in order not to endanger the vessel's safety I have had to put her about and run before the storm."

"That will cause us a most lamentable delay!" said Godfrey.

"Very much so," answered Captain Turcott, "but when day breaks, if the sea falls a little, I shall resume our westerly route. I should recommend you, Mr. Godfrey, to get back to your cabin. Take my advice, try and sleep while we are running before the wind. You will be less knocked about."

Godfrey made a sign of affirmation; turning a last anxious glance at the low clouds which were chasing each other with extreme swiftness, he left the bridge, returned to his cabin, and soon resumed his interrupted slumbers. The next morning, the 22nd of

June, as Captain Turcott had said, the wind having sensibly abated, the *Dream* was headed in proper direction.

This navigation towards the west during the day, towards the east during the night, lasted for forty-eight hours more; but the barometer showed some tendency to rise, its oscillations became less frequent; it was to be presumed that the bad weather would end in northerly winds. And so in fact it happened.

On the 25th of June, about eight o'clock in the morning, when Godfrey stepped on deck, a charming breeze from the north-east had swept away the clouds, the sun's rays were shining through the rigging and tipping its projecting points with touches of fire. The sea, deep green in colour, glittered along a large section of its surface beneath the direct influence of its beams. The wind blew only in feeble gusts which laced the wave-crests with delicate foam. The lower sails were set.

Properly speaking, they were not regular waves on which the sea rose and fell, but only lengthened undulations which gently rocked the steamer.

Undulations or waves, it is true, it was all one to Professor Tartlet, as unwell when it was "too mild," as when it was "too rough." There he was, half crouching on the deck, with his mouth open like a carp fainted out of water.

The mate on the poop, his telescope at his eye, was looking towards the north-east.

Godfrey approached him.

"Well, sir," said he gaily, "to-day is a little better than yesterday."

"Yes, Mr. Godfrey," replied the mate, "we are now in smooth water."

"And the *Dream* is on the right road!"

"Not yet."

"Not yet? and why?"

"Because we have evidently drifted north-eastwards during this last spell, and we must find out our position exactly."

"But there is a good sun and a horizon perfectly clear."

"At noon in taking its height we shall get a good observation, and then the captain will give us our course."

"Where is the captain?" asked Godfrey.

"He has gone off."

"Gone off?"

"Yes! our look-outs saw from the whiteness of the sea that there were some breakers away to the east; breakers which are not shown on the chart. So the steam launch was got out, and with

38

the boatswain and three men, Captain Turcott has gone off to explore."

"How long ago?"

"About an hour and a half!"

"Ah!" said Godfrey, "I am sorry he did not tell me. I should like to have gone too."

"You were asleep, Mr. Godfrey," replied the mate, "and the captain did not like to wake you."

"I am sorry; but tell me, which way did the launch go?"

"Over there," answered the mate, "over the starboard bow, north-eastwards."

"And can you see it with the telescope?"

"No, she is too far off."

"But will she be long before she comes back?"

"She won't be long, for the captain is going to take the sights himself, and to do that he must be back before noon."

At this Godfrey went and sat on the forecastle, having sent some one for his glasses. He was anxious to watch the return of the launch. Captain Turcott's reconnaissance did not cause him any surprise. It was natural that the *Dream* should not be run into danger on a part of the sea where breakers had been reported.

Two hours passed. It was not until half-past ten that a light line of smoke began to rise on the horizon.

It was evidently the steam launch which, having finished the reconnaissance, was making for the ship.

It amused Godfrey to follow her in the field of his glasses. He saw her little by little reveal herself in clearer outline, he saw her grow on the surface of the sea, and then give definite shape to her smoke wreath, as it mingled with a few curls of steam on the clear depth of the horizon.

She was an excellent little vessel, of immense speed, and as she came along at full steam, she was soon visible to the naked eye. Towards eleven o'clock, the wash from her bow as she tore through the waves was perfectly distinct, and behind her the long furrow of foam gradually growing wider and fainter like the tail of a comet.

At a quarter-past eleven, Captain Turcott hailed and boarded the *Dream*.

"Well, captain, what news?" asked Godfrey, shaking his hand.

"Ah! Good morning, Mr. Godfrey!"

"And the breakers?"

"Only show!" answered Captain Turcott. "We saw nothing suspicious, our men must have been deceived, but I am rather surprised at that, all the same."

39

"We are going ahead then?" said Godfrey.

"Yes, we are going on now, but I must first take an observation."

"Shall we get the launch on board?" asked the mate.

"No," answered the captain, "we may want it again. Leave it in tow!"

The captain's orders were executed, and the launch, still under steam, dropped round to the stern of the *Dream*.

Three-quarters of an hour afterwards, Captain Turcott, with his sextant in his hand, took the sun's altitude, and having made his observation, he gave the course. That done, having given a last look at the horizon, he called the mate, and taking him into his cabin, the two remained there in a long consultation.

The day was a very fine one. The sails had been furled, and the *Dream* steamed rapidly without their help. The wind was very slight, and with the speed given by the screw there would not have been enough to fill them.

Godfrey was thoroughly happy. This sailing over a beautiful sea, under a beautiful sky, could anything be more cheering, could anything give more impulse to thought, more satisfaction to the mind? And it is scarcely to be wondered at that Professor Tartlet also began to recover himself a little. The state of the sea did not inspire him with immediate inquietude, and his physical being showed a little reaction. He tried to eat, but without taste or appetite. Godfrey would have had him take off the life-belt which encircled his waist, but this he absolutely refused to do. Was there not a chance of this conglomeration of wood and iron, which men call a vessel, gaping asunder at any moment.

The evening came, a thick mist spread over the sky, without descending to the level of the sea. The night was to be much darker than would have been thought from the magnificent daytime.

There was no rock to fear in these parts, for Captain Turcott had just fixed his exact position on the charts; but collisions are always possible, and they are much more frequent on foggy nights.

The lamps were carefully put into place as soon as the sun set. The white one was run up the mast, and the green light to the right and the red one to the left gleamed in the shrouds. If the *Dream* was run down, at the least it would not be her fault—that was one consolation. To founder even when one is in order is to founder nevertheless, and if any one on board made this observation it was of course Professor Tartlet. However, the worthy man, always on the roll and the pitch, had regained his cabin, Godfrey his; the one with the assurance, the other in the hope that he would pass a good night, for the *Dream* scarcely moved on the crest of the lengthened waves.

Captain Turcott, having handed over the watch to the mate, also came under the poop to take a few hours' rest. All was in order. The steamer could go ahead in perfect safety, although it did not seem as though the thick fog would lift.

In about twenty minutes Godfrey was asleep, and the sleepless Tartlet, who had gone to bed with his clothes on as usual, only betrayed himself by distant sighs. All at once—at about one in the morning—Godfrey was awakened by a dreadful clamour.

He jumped out of bed, slipped on his clothes, his trousers, his waistcoat and his sea-boots.

Almost immediately a fearful cry was heard on deck, "We are sinking! we are sinking!"

In an instant Godfrey was out of his cabin and in the saloon. There he cannoned against an inert mass which he did not recognize. It was Professor Tartlet.

The whole crew were on deck, hurrying about at the orders of the mate and captain.

"A collision?" asked Godfrey.

"I don't know, I don't know—this beastly fog—" answered the mate; "but we are sinking!"

"Sinking?" exclaimed Godfrey.

And in fact the *Dream*, which had doubtless struck on a rock was sensibly foundering. The water was creeping up to the level of the deck. The engine fires were probably already out below.

"To the sea! to the sea, Mr. Morgan!" exclaimed the captain. "There is not a moment to lose! You can see the ship settling down! It will draw you down in the eddy!"

"And Tartlet?"

"I'll look after him!—We are only half a cable from the shore!"

"But you?"

"My duty compels me to remain here to the last, and I remain!" said the captain. "But get off! get off!"

Godfrey still hesitated to cast himself into the waves, but the water was already up to the level of the deck.

Captain Turcott knowing that Godfrey swam like a fish, seized him by the shoulders, and did him the service of throwing him overboard.

It was time! Had it not been for the darkness, there would doubtless have been seen a deep raging vortex in the place once occupied by the *Dream*.

But Godfrey, in a few strokes in the calm water, was able to

41

get swiftly clear of the whirlpool, which would have dragged him down like the maelstrom.

All this was the work of a minute.

A few minutes afterwards, amid shouts of despair, the lights on board went out one after the other.

Doubt existed no more; the *Dream* had sunk head downwards!

As for Godfrey he had been able to reach a large lofty rock away from the surf. There, shouting vainly in the darkness, hearing no voice in reply to his own, not knowing if he should find himself on an isolated rock or at the extremity of a line of reefs, and perhaps the sole survivor of the catastrophe, he waited for the dawn.

CHAPTER VIII

WHICH LEADS GODFREY TO BITTER REFLECTIONS ON THE MANIA FOR TRAVELLING

Three long hours had still to pass before the sun reappeared above the horizon. These were such hours that they might rather be called centuries.

The trial was a rough one to begin with, but, we repeat, Godfrey had not come out for a simple promenade. He himself put it very well when he said he had left behind him quite a lifetime of happiness and repose, which he would never find again in his search for adventures. He tried his utmost therefore to rise to the situation.

He was, temporarily, under shelter. The sea after all could not drive him off the rock which lay anchored alone amid the spray of the surf. Was there any fear of the incoming tide soon reaching him? No, for on reflection he concluded that the wreck had taken place at the highest tide of the new moon.

But was the rock isolated? Did it command a line of breakers scattered on this portion of the sea? What was this coast which Captain Turcott had thought he saw in the darkness? To which continent did it belong? It was only too certain that the *Dream* had been driven out of her route during the storm of the preceding days. The position of the ship could not have been exactly fixed. How could there be a doubt of this when the captain had two hours before affirmed that his charts bore no indication of breakers in these parts! He had even done better and had gone himself to reconnoitre these imaginary reefs which his look-outs had reported they had seen in the east.

It nevertheless had been only too true, and Captain Turcott's reconnaissance would have certainly prevented the catastrophe if it had only been pushed far enough. But what was the good of returning to the past?

The important question in face of what had happened—a question of life or death—was for Godfrey to know if he was near to some land. In what part of the Pacific there would be time later on to determine. Before everything he must think as soon as the day came of how to leave the rock, which in its biggest part could not measure more that twenty yards square. But people do not leave one place except to go to another. And if this other did not exist, if the captain had been deceived in the fog, if around the breakers there stretched a boundless sea, if at the extreme point of view the sky and the water seemed to meet all round the horizon?

The thoughts of the young man were thus concentrated on this point. All his powers of vision did he employ to discover through the black night if any confused mass, any heap of rocks or cliffs, would reveal the neighbourhood of land to the eastward of the reef.

Godfrey saw nothing. Not a smell of earth reached his nose, not a sensation of light reached his eyes, not a sound reached his ears. Not a bird traversed the darkness. It seemed that around him there was nothing but a vast desert of water.

Godfrey did not hide from himself that the chances were a thousand to one that he was lost. He no longer thought of making the tour of the world, but of facing death, and calmly and bravely his thoughts rose to that Providence which can do all things for the feeblest of its creatures, though the creatures can do nothing of themselves. And so Godfrey had to wait for the day to resign himself to his fate, if safety was impossible; and, on the contrary, to try everything, if there was any chance of life.

Calmed by the very gravity of his reflections, Godfrey had seated himself on the rock. He had stripped off some of his clothes which had been saturated by the sea-water, his woollen waistcoat and his heavy boots, so as to be ready to jump into the sea if necessary.

However, was it possible that no one had survived the wreck? What! not one of the men of the *Dream* carried to shore? Had they all been sucked in by the terrible whirlpool which the ship had drawn round herself as she sank? The last to whom Godfrey had spoken was Captain Turcott, resolved not to quit his ship while one of his sailors was still there! It was the captain himself who had hurled him into the sea at the moment the *Dream* was disappearing.

But the others, the unfortunate Tartlet, and the unhappy Chinese, surprised without doubt, and swallowed up, the one in the poop, the other in the depths of the hold, what had become of them? Of all those on board the *Dream*, was he the only one saved? And had the steam launch remained at the stern of the steamer? Could not a few passengers or sailors have saved themselves therein, and found time to flee from the wreck? But was it not rather to be feared that the launch had been dragged down by the ship under several fathoms of water?

Godfrey then said to himself, that if in this dark night he could not see, he could at least make himself heard. There was nothing to prevent his shouting and hailing in the deep silence. Perhaps the voice of one of his companions would respond to his.

Over and over again then did he call, giving forth a prolonged shout which should have been heard for a considerable distance round. Not a cry answered to his.

He began again, many times, turning successively to every point of the horizon.

Absolute silence.

"Alone! alone!" he murmured.

Not only had no cry answered to his, but no echo had sent him back the sound of his own voice. Had he been near a cliff, not far from a group of rocks, such as generally border the shore, it was certain that his shouts, repelled by the obstacles, would have returned to him. Either eastwards of the reef, therefore, stretched a low-lying shore ill-adapted for the production of an echo, or there was no land in his vicinity, the bed of breakers on which he had found refuge was isolated.

Three hours were passed in these anxieties. Godfrey, quite chilled, walked about the top of the rock, trying to battle with the cold. At last a few pale beams of light tinged the clouds in the zenith. It was the reflection of the first colouring of the horizon.

Godfrey turned to this side—the only one towards which there could be land—to see if any cliff outlined itself in the shadow. With its early rays the rising sun might disclose its features more distinctly.

But nothing appeared through the misty dawn. A light fog was rising over the sea, which did not even admit of his discovering the extent of the breakers.

He had, therefore, to satisfy himself with illusions. If Godfrey were really cast on an isolated rock in the Pacific, it was death to him after a brief delay, death by hunger, by thirst, or if necessary, death at the bottom of the sea as a last resource!

However, he kept constantly looking, and it seemed as though the intensity of his gaze increased enormously, for all his will was concentrated therein.

At length the morning mist began to fade away. Godfrey saw the rocks which formed the reef successively defined in relief on the sea, like a troop of marine monsters. It was a long and irregular assemblage of dark boulders, strangely worn, of all sizes and forms, whose direction was almost west and east. The enormous block on the top of which Godfrey found himself emerged from the sea on the western edge of the bank scarcely thirty fathoms from the spot where the *Dream* had gone down. The sea hereabouts appeared to

45

be very deep, for of the steamer nothing was to be seen, not even the ends of her masts. Perhaps by some under-current she had been drawn away from the reefs.

A glance was enough for Godfrey to take in this state of affairs. There was no safety on that side. All his attention was directed towards the other side of the breakers, which the lifting fog was gradually disclosing. The sea, now that the tide had retired, allowed the rocks to stand out very distinctly. They could be seen to lengthen as there humid bases widened. Here were vast intervals of water, there a few shallow pools. If they joined on to any coast, it would not be difficult to reach it.

Up to the present, however, there was no sign of any shore. Nothing yet indicated the proximity of dry land, even in this direction.

The fog continued to lift, and the field of view persistently watched by Godfrey continued to grow. Its wreaths had now rolled off for about half a mile or so. Already a few sandy flats appeared among the rocks, carpeted with their slimy sea-weed.

Did not this sand indicate more or less the presence of a beach, and if the beach existed, could there be a doubt but what it belonged to the coast of a more important land? At length a long profile of low hills, buttressed with huge granitic rocks, became clearly outlined and seemed to shut in the horizon on the east. The sun had drunk up all the morning vapours, and his disc broke forth in all its glory.

"Land! land!" exclaimed Godfrey.

And he stretched his hands towards the shore-line, as he knelt on the reef and offered his thanks to Heaven.

It was really land. The breakers only formed a projecting ridge, something like the southern cape of a bay, which curved round for about two miles or more. The bottom of the curve seemed to be a level beach, bordered by trifling hills, contoured here and there with lines of vegetation, but of no great size.

From the place which Godfrey occupied, his view was able to grasp the whole of this side.

Bordered north and south by two unequal promontories, it stretched away for, at the most, five or six miles. It was possible, however, that it formed part of a large district. Whatever it was, it offered at the least temporary safety. Godfrey, at the sight, could not conceive a doubt but that he had not been thrown on to a solitary reef, and that this morsel of ground would satisfy his earliest wants.

"To land! to land!" he said to himself.

But before he left the reef, he gave a look round for the last time. His eyes again interrogated the sea away up to the horizon. Would some raft appear on the surface of the waves, some fragment of the *Dream*, some survivor, perhaps?

Nothing. The launch even was not there, and had probably been dragged into the common abyss.

Then the idea occurred to Godfrey that among the breakers some of his companions might have found a refuge, and were, like him, waiting for the day to try and reach the shore.

There was nobody, neither on the rocks, nor on the beach! The reef was as deserted as the ocean!

But in default of survivors, had not the sea thrown up some of the corpses? Could not Godfrey find among the rocks, along to the utmost boundary of the surf, the inanimate bodies of some of his companions?

No! Nothing along the whole length of the breakers, which the last ripples of the ebb had now left bare.

Godfrey was alone! He could only count on himself to battle with the dangers of every sort which environed him!

Before this reality, however, Godfrey, let it be said to his credit, did not quail. But as before everything it was best for him to ascertain the nature of the ground from which he was separated by so short a distance, he left the summit of the rock and began to approach the shore.

When the interval which separated the rocks was too great to be cleared at a bound, he got down into the water, and sometimes walking and sometimes swimming he easily gained the one next in order. When there was but a yard or two between, he jumped from one rock to the other. His progress over these slimy stones, carpeted with glistening sea-weeds, was not easy, and it was long. Nearly a quarter of a mile had thus to be traversed.

But Godfrey was active and handy, and at length he set foot on the land where there probably awaited him, if not early death, at least a miserable life worse than death. Hunger, thirst, cold, and nakedness, and perils of all kinds; without a weapon of defence, without a gun to shoot with, without a change of clothes—such the extremities to which he was reduced.

How imprudent he had been! He had been desirous of knowing if he was capable of making his way in the world under difficult circumstances! He had put himself to the proof! He had envied the lot of a Crusoe! Well, he would see if the lot were an enviable one!

And then there returned to his mind the thought of his happy existence, that easy life in San Francisco, in the midst of a rich and

47

loving family, which he had abandoned to throw himself into adventures. He thought of his Uncle Will, of his betrothed Phina, of his friends who would doubtless never see him again.

As he called up these remembrances his heart swelled, and in spite of his resolution a tear rose to his eyes.

And again, if he was not alone, if some other survivor of the shipwreck had managed, like him, to reach the shore, and even in default of the captain or the mate, this proved to be Professor Tartlet, how little he could depend on that frivolous being, and how slightly improved the chances of the future appeared! At this point, however, he still had hope. If he had found no trace among the breakers, would he meet with any on the beach?

Who else but he had already touched the shore, seeking a companion who was seeking him?

Godfrey took another long look from north to south. He did not notice a single human being. Evidently this portion of the earth was uninhabited. In any case there was no sign, not a trace of smoke in the air, not a vestige.

"Let us get on!" said Godfrey to himself.

And he walked along the beach towards the north, before venturing to climb the sand dunes, which would allow him to reconnoitre the country over a larger extent.

The silence was absolute. The sand had received no other footmark. A few sea-birds, gulls or guillemots, were skimming along the edge of the rocks, the only living things in the solitude.

Godfrey continued his walk for a quarter of an hour. At last he was about to turn on to the talus of the most elevated of the dunes, dotted with rushes and brushwood, when he suddenly stopped.

A shapeless object, extraordinarily distended, something like the corpse of a sea monster, thrown there, doubtless, by the late storm, was lying about thirty paces off on the edge of the reef.

Godfrey hastened to run towards it.

The nearer he approached the more rapidly did his heart beat. In truth, in this stranded animal he seemed to recognize a human form.

Godfrey was not ten paces away from it, when he stopped as if rooted to the soil, and exclaimed,—

"Tartlet!"

It was the professor of dancing and deportment.

Godfrey rushed towards his companion, who perhaps still breathed.

A moment afterwards he saw that it was the life-belt which

produced this extraordinary distension, and gave the aspect of a monster of the sea to the unfortunate professor.

But although Tartlet was motionless, was he dead? Perhaps this natatory clothing had kept him above water, while the surf had borne him to shore?

Godfrey set to work. He knelt down by Tartlet; he unloosed the life-belt and rubbed him vigorously. He noticed at last a light breath on the half-opened lips! He put his hand on his heart! The heart still beat.

Godfrey spoke to him.

Tartlet shook his head, then he gave utterance to a hoarse exclamation, followed by incoherent words.

Godfrey shook him violently.

Tartlet then opened his eyes, passed his left hand over his brow, lifted his right hand and assured himself that his precious kit and bow, which he tightly held, had not abandoned him.

"Tartlet! My dear Tartlet!" shouted Godfrey, lightly raising his head.

The head with his mass of tumbled hair gave an affirmative nod.

"It is I! I! Godfrey!"

"Godfrey?" asked the professor.

And then he turned over, and rose on to his knees, and looked about, and smiled, and rose to his feet! He had discovered that at last he was on a solid base! He had gathered that he was no longer on the ship's deck, exposed to all the uncertainties of its pitches and its rolls! The sea had ceased to carry him! He stood on firm ground!

And then Professor Tartlet recovered the aplomb which he had lost since his departure; his feet placed themselves naturally, with their toes turned out, in the regulation position; his left hand seized his kit, his right hand grasped his bow.

Then, while the strings, vigorously attacked, gave forth a humid sound of melancholy sonorousness, these words escaped his smiling lips,—

"In place, miss!"

The good man was thinking of Phina.

49

CHAPTER IX

IN WHICH IT IS SHOWN THAT CRUSOES DO NOT HAVE
EVERYTHING AS THEY WISH

That done, the professor and his pupil rushed into one another's arms.

"My dear Godfrey!" exclaimed Tartlet.

"My good Tartlet!" replied Godfrey.

"At last we are arrived in port!" observed the professor in the tone of a man who had had enough of navigation and its accidents.

He called it arriving in port!

Godfrey had no desire to contradict him.

"Take off your life-belt," he said. "It suffocates you and hampers your movements."

"Do you think I can do so without inconvenience?" asked Tartlet.

"Without any inconvenience," answered Godfrey. "Now put up your fiddle, and let us take a look round."

"Come on," replied the professor; "but if you don't mind, Godfrey, let us go to the first restaurant we see. I am dying of hunger, and a dozen sandwiches washed down with a glass or two of wine will soon set me on my legs again."

"Yes! to the first restaurant!" answered Godfrey, nodding his head; "and even to the last, if the first does not suit us."

"And," continued Tartlet, "we can ask some fellow as we go along the road to the telegraph office so as to send a message off to your Uncle Kolderup. That excellent man will hardly refuse to send on some necessary cash for us to get back to Montgomery Street, for I have not got a cent with me!"

"Agreed, to the first telegraph office," answered Godfrey, "or if there isn't one in this country, to the first post office. Come on, Tartlet."

The professor took off his swimming apparatus, and passed it over his shoulder like a hunting-horn, and then both stepped out for the edge of the dunes which bordered the shore.

What more particularly interested Godfrey, whom the encounter with Tartlet had imbued with some hope, was to see if they too were the only survivors of the *Dream*.

A quarter of an hour after the explorers had left the edge of the reef they had climbed a dune about sixty or eighty feet high, and stood on its crest. Thence they looked on a large extent of coast, and examined the horizon in the east, which till then had been hidden by the hills on the shore.

Two or three miles away in that direction a second line of hills formed the background, and beyond them nothing was seen of the horizon.

Towards the north the coast trended off to a point, but it could not be seen if there was a corresponding cape behind. On the south a creek ran some distance into the shore, and on this side it looked as though the ocean closed the view. Whence this land in the Pacific was probably a peninsula, and the isthmus which joined it to the continent would have to be sought for towards the north or north-east.

The country, however, far from being barren, was hidden beneath an agreeable mantle of verdure; long prairies, amid which meandered many limpid streams, and high and thick forests, whose trees rose above one another to the very background of hills. It was a charming landscape.

But of houses forming town, village, or hamlet, not one was in sight! Of buildings grouped and arranged as a farm of any sort, not a sign! Of smoke in the sky, betraying some dwelling hidden among the trees, not a trace. Not a steeple above the branches, not a windmill on an isolated hill. Not even in default of houses a cabin, a hut, an ajoupa, or a wigwam? No! nothing. If human beings inhabited this unknown land, they must live like troglodytes, below, and not above the ground. Not a road was visible, not a footpath, not even a track. It seemed that the foot of man had never trod either a rock of the beach or a blade of the grass on the prairies.

"I don't see the town," remarked Tartlet, who, however, remained on tiptoe.

"That is perhaps because it is not in this part of the province!" answered Godfrey.

"But a village?"

"There's nothing here."

"Where are we then?"

"I know nothing about it."

"What! You don't know! But Godfrey, we had better make haste and find out."

"Who is to tell us?"

"What will become of us then?" exclaimed Tartlet, rounding his arms and lifting them to the sky.

"Become a couple of Crusoes!"

51

At this answer the professor gave a bound such as no clown had ever equalled.

Crusoes! They! A Crusoe! He! Descendants of that Selkirk who had lived for long years on the island of Juan Fernandez! Imitators of the imaginary heroes of Daniel Defoe and De Wyss whose adventures they had so often read! Abandoned, far from their relatives, their friends; separated from their fellow-men by thousands of miles, destined to defend their lives perhaps against wild beasts, perhaps against savages who would land there, wretches without resources, suffering from hunger, suffering from thirst, without weapons, without tools, almost without clothes, left to themselves. No, it was impossible!

"Don't say such things, Godfrey," exclaimed Tartlet. "No! Don't joke about such things! The mere supposition will kill me! You are laughing at me, are you not?"

"Yes, my gallant Tartlet," answered Godfrey. "Reassure yourself. But in the first place, let us think about matters that are pressing."

In fact, they had to try and find some cavern, a grotto or hole, in which to pass the night, and then to collect some edible mollusks so as to satisfy the cravings of their stomachs.

Godfrey and Tartlet then commenced to descend the talus of the dunes in the direction of the reef. Godfrey showed himself very ardent in his researches, and Tartlet considerably stupefied by his shipwreck experiences. The first looked before him, behind him, and all around him; the second hardly saw ten paces in front of him.

"If there are no inhabitants on this land, are there any animals?" asked Godfrey.

He meant to say domestic animals, such as furred and feathered game, not wild animals which abound in tropical regions, and with which they were not likely to have to do.

Several flocks of birds were visible on the shore, bitterns, curlews, bernicle geese, and teal, which hovered and chirped and filled the air with their flutterings and cries, doubtless protesting against the invasion of their domain.

Godfrey was justified in concluding that where there were birds there were nests, and where there were nests there were eggs. The birds congregated here in such numbers, because rocks provided them with thousands of cavities for their dwelling-places. In the distance a few herons and some flocks of snipe indicated the neighbourhood of a marsh.

Birds then were not wanting, the only difficulty was to get at them without fire-arms. The best thing to do now was to make use of them in the egg state, and consume them under that elementary but nourishing form.

But if the dinner was there, how were they to cook it? How were they to set about lighting a fire? An important question, the solution of which was postponed.

Godfrey and Tartlet returned straight towards the reef, over which some sea-birds were circling. An agreeable surprise there awaited them.

Among the indigenous fowl which ran along the sand of the beach and pecked about among the sea-weed and under the tufts of aquatic plants, was it a dozen hens and two or three cocks of the American breed that they beheld? No! There was no mistake, for at their approach did not a resounding cock-a-doodle-do-oo-oo rend the air like the sound of a trumpet?

And farther off, what were those quadrupeds which were gliding in and out of the rocks, and making their way towards the first slopes of the hills, or grubbing beneath some of the green shrubs? Godfrey could not be mistaken. There were a dozen agouties, five or six sheep, and as many goats, who were quietly browsing on the first vegetation on the very edge of the prairie.

"Look there, Tartlet!" he exclaimed.

And the professor looked, but saw nothing, so much was he absorbed with the thought of this unexpected situation.

A thought flashed across the mind of Godfrey, and it was correct: it was that these hens, agouties, goats, and sheep had belonged to the *Dream*. At the moment she went down, the fowls had easily been able to reach the reef and then the beach. As for the quadrupeds, they could easily have swum ashore.

"And so," remarked Godfrey, "what none of our unfortunate companions have been able to do, these simple animals, guided by their instinct, have done! And of all those on board the *Dream*, none have been saved but a few beasts!"

"Including ourselves!" answered Tartlet naively.

As far as he was concerned, he had come ashore unconsciously, very much like one of the animals. It mattered little. It was a very fortunate thing for the two shipwrecked men that a certain number of these animals had reached the shore. They would collect them, fold them, and with the special fecundity of their species, if their stay on this land was a lengthy one, it would be easy to have quite a flock of quadrupeds, and a yard full of poultry.

But on this occasion, Godfrey wished to keep to such alimentary resources as the coast could furnish, either in eggs or shell-fish. Professor Tartlet and he set to work to forage among the

53

interstices of the stones, and beneath the carpet of sea-weeds, and not without success. They soon collected quite a notable quantity of mussels and periwinkles, which they could eat raw. A few dozen eggs of the bernicle geese were also found among the higher rocks which shut in the bay on the north. They had enough to satisfy a good many; and, hunger pressing, Godfrey and Tartlet hardly thought of making difficulties about their first repast.

"And the fire?" said the professor.

"Yes! The fire!" said Godfrey.

It was the most serious of questions, and it led to an inventory being made of the contents of their pockets. Those of the professor were empty or nearly so. They contained a few spare strings for his kit, and a piece of rosin for his bow. How would you get a light from that, I should like to know? Godfrey was hardly better provided. However, it was with extreme satisfaction that he discovered in his pocket an excellent knife, whose leather case had kept it from the sea-water. This knife, with blade, gimlet, hook, and saw, was a valuable instrument under the circumstances. But besides this tool, Godfrey and his companion had only their two hands; and as the hands of the professor had never been used except in playing his fiddle, and making his gestures, Godfrey concluded that he would have to trust to his own.

He thought, however, of utilizing those of Tartlet for procuring a fire by means of rubbing two sticks of wood rapidly together. A few eggs cooked in the embers would be greatly appreciated at their second meal at noon.

While Godfrey then was occupied in robbing the nests in spite of the proprietors, who tried to defend their progeny in the shell, the professor went off to collect some pieces of wood which had been dried by the sun at the foot of the dunes. These were taken behind a rock sheltered from the wind from the sea. Tartlet then chose two very dry pieces, with the intention of gradually obtaining sufficient heat by rubbing them vigorously and continuously together. What simple Polynesian savages commonly did, why should not the professor, so much their superior in his own opinion, be able to do?

Behold him then, rubbing and rubbing, in a way to dislocate the muscles of his arm and shoulder. He worked himself into quite a rage, poor man! But whether it was that the wood was not right, or its dryness was not sufficient, or the professor held it wrongly, or had not got the peculiar turn of hand necessary for operations of this kind, if he did not get much heat out of the wood, he succeeded in getting a good deal out of himself. In short, it was his own forehead alone which smoked under the vapours of his own perspiration.

When Godfrey returned with his collection of eggs, he found Tartlet in a rage, in a state to which his choregraphic exercises had never doubtless provoked him.

"Doesn't it do?" he asked.

"No, Godfrey, it does not do," replied the professor. "And I begin to think that these inventions of the savages are only imaginations to deceive the world."

"No," answered Godfrey. "But in that, as in all things, you must know how to do it."

"These eggs, then?"

"There is another way. If you attach one of these eggs to the end of a string and whirl it round rapidly, and suddenly arrest the movement of rotation, the movement may perhaps transform itself into heat, and then—"

"And then the egg will be cooked?"

"Yes, if the rotation has been swift enough and the stoppage sudden enough. But how do you produce the stoppage without breaking the egg? Now, there is a simpler way, dear Tartlet. Behold!"

And carefully taking one of the eggs of the bernicle goose, he broke the shell at its end, and adroitly swallowed the inside without any further formalities.

Tartlet could not make up his mind to imitate him, and contented himself with the shell-fish.

It now remained to look for a grotto or some shelter in which to pass the night.

"It is an unheard-of thing," observed the professor, "that Crusoes cannot at the least find a cavern, which, later on, they can make their home!"

"Let us look," said Godfrey.

It was unheard of. We must avow, however, that on this occasion the tradition was broken. In vain did they search along the rocky shore on the southern part of the bay. Not a cavern, not a grotto, not a hole was there that would serve as a shelter. They had to give up the idea. Godfrey resolved to reconnoitre up to the first trees in the background beyond the sandy coast.

Tartlet and he then remounted the first line of sandhills and crossed the verdant prairies which they had seen a few hours before.

A very odd circumstance, and a very fortunate one at the time, that the other survivors of the wreck voluntarily followed them. Evidently, cocks and hens, and sheep, goats and agouties, driven by instinct, had resolved to go with them. Doubtless they felt too lonely on the beach, which did not yield sufficient food.

Three-quarters of an hour later Godfrey and Tartlet—they had scarcely spoken during the exploration—arrived at the outskirt of the trees. Not a trace was there of habitation or inhabitant. Complete solitude. It might even be doubted if this part of the country had ever been trodden by human feet.

In this place were a few handsome trees, in isolated groups, and others more crowded about a quarter of a mile in the rear formed a veritable forest of different species.

Godfrey looked out for some old trunk, hollowed by age, which could offer a shelter among its branches, but his researches were in vain, although he continued them till night was falling.

Hunger made itself sharply felt, and the two contented themselves with mussels, of which they had thoughtfully brought an ample supply from the beach. Then, quite tired out, they lay down at the foot of a tree, and trusting to Providence, slept through the night.

CHAPTER X

IN WHICH GODFREY DOES WHAT ANY OTHER SHIPWRECKED MAN WOULD HAVE DONE UNDER THE CIRCUMSTANCES

The night passed without incident. The two men, quite knocked up with excitement and fatigue, had slept as peacefully as if they had been in the most comfortable room in the mansion in Montgomery Street.

On the morrow, the 27th of June, at the first rays of the rising sun, the crow of the cock awakened them.

Godfrey immediately recognized where he was, but Tartlet had to rub his eyes and stretch his arms for some time before he did so.

"Is breakfast this morning to resemble dinner yesterday?" was his first observation.

"I am afraid so," answered Godfrey. "But I hope we shall dine better this evening."

The professor could not restrain a significant grimace. Where were the tea and sandwiches which had hitherto been brought to him when he awoke? How could he wait till breakfast-time, the bell for which would perhaps never sound, without this preparatory repast?

But it was necessary to make a start. Godfrey felt the responsibility which rested on him, on him alone, for he could in no way depend on his companion. In that empty box which served the professor for a cranium there could be born no practical idea; Godfrey would have to think, contrive, and decide for both.

His first thought was for Phina, his betrothed, whom he had so stupidly refused to make his wife; his second for his Uncle Will, whom he had so imprudently left, and then turning to Tartlet,—

"To vary our ordinary," he said, "here are some shell-fish and half a dozen eggs."

"And nothing to cook them with!"

"Nothing!" said Godfrey. "But if the food itself was missing, what would you say then, Tartlet?"

"I should say that nothing was not enough," said Tartlet drily.

Nevertheless, they had to be content with this repast.

The very natural idea occurred to Godfrey to push forward the reconnaissance commenced the previous evening. Above all it was

57

necessary to know as soon as possible in what part of the Pacific Ocean the *Dream* had been lost, so as to discover some inhabited place on the shore, where they could either arrange the way of returning home or await the passing of some ship.

Godfrey observed that if he could cross the second line of hills, whose picturesque outline was visible beyond the first, that he might perhaps be able to do this. He reckoned that they could get there in an hour or two, and it was to this urgent exploration that he resolved to devote the first hours of the day. He looked round him. The cocks and hens were beginning to peck about among the high vegetation. Agouties, goats, sheep, went and came on the skirt of the forest.

Godfrey did not care to drag all this flock of poultry and quadrupeds about with him. But to keep them more safely in this place, it would be necessary to leave Tartlet in charge of them.

Tartlet agreed to remain alone, and for several hours to act as shepherd of the flock.

He made but one observation,—

"If you lose yourself, Godfrey?"

"Have no fear of that," answered the young man, "I have only this forest to cross, and as you will not leave its edge I am certain to find you again."

"Don't forget the telegram to your Uncle Will, and ask him for a good many hundred dollars."

"The telegram—or the letter! It is all one!" answered Godfrey, who so long as he had not fixed on the position of this land was content to leave Tartlet to his illusions.

Then having shaken hands with the professor, he plunged beneath the trees, whose thick branches scarcely allowed the sun's rays to penetrate. It was their direction, however, which was to guide our young explorer towards the high hill whose curtain hid from his view the whole of the eastern horizon.

Footpath there was none. The ground, however, was not free from all imprint. Godfrey in certain places remarked the tracks of animals. On two or three occasions he even believed he saw some rapid ruminants moving off, either elans, deer, or wapiti, but he recognized no trace of ferocious animals such as tigers or jaguars, whose absence, however, was no cause for regret.

The first floor of the forest, that is to say all that portion of the trees comprised between the first fork and the branches, afforded an asylum to a great number of birds—wild pigeons by the hundred beneath the trees, ospreys, grouse, aracaris with beaks like a lobster's claw, and higher, hovering above the glades, two or three of those lammergeiers whose eye resembles a cockade. But none of the birds were of such special kinds that he could therefrom make out the latitude of this continent.

So it was with the trees of this forest. Almost the same species as those in that part of the United States which comprises Lower California, the Bay of Monterey, and New Mexico.

Arbutus-trees, large-flowered cornels, maples, birches, oaks, four or five varieties of magnolias and sea-pines, such as are met with in South Carolina, then in the centre of vast clearances, olive-trees, chestnuts, and small shrubs. Tufts of tamarinds, myrtles, and mastic-trees, such as are produced in the temperate zone. Generally, there was enough space between the trees to allow him to pass without being obliged to call on fire or the axe. The sea breeze circulated freely amid the higher branches, and here and there great patches of light shone on the ground.

And so Godfrey went along striking an oblique line beneath these large trees. To take any precautions never occurred to him. The desire to reach the heights which bordered the forest on the east entirely absorbed him. He sought among the foliage for the direction of the solar rays so as to march straight on his goal. He did not even see the guide-birds, so named because they fly before the steps of the traveller, stopping, returning, and darting on ahead as if they were showing the way. Nothing could distract him.

His state of mind was intelligible. Before an hour had elapsed his fate would be settled! Before an hour he would know if it were possible to reach some inhabited portion of the continent.

Already Godfrey, reasoning on what had been the route followed and the way made by the *Dream* during a navigation of seventeen days, had concluded that it could only be on the Japanese or Chinese coast that the ship had gone down.

Besides the position of the sun, always in the south, rendered it quite certain that the *Dream* had not crossed the line.

Two hours after he had started Godfrey reckoned the distance he had travelled at about five miles, considering several circuits which he had had to make owing to the density of the forest. The second group of hills could not be far away.

Already the trees were getting farther apart from each other, forming isolated groups, and the rays of light penetrated more easily through the lofty branches. The ground began slightly to slope, and then abruptly to rise.

Although he was somewhat fatigued, Godfrey had enough will not to slacken his pace. He would doubtless have run had it not been for the steepness of the earlier ascents.

He had soon got high enough to overlook the general mass of the verdant dome which stretched away behind him, and whence several heads of trees here and there emerged.

But Godfrey did not dream of looking back. His eyes never quitted the line of the denuded ridge, which showed itself about 400 or 500 feet before and above him. That was the barrier which all the time hid him from the eastern horizon.

A tiny cone, obliquely truncated, overlooked this rugged line and joined on with its gentle slope to the sinuous crest of the hills.

"There! there!" said Godfrey, "that is the point I must reach! The top of that cone! And from there what shall I see?—A town?—A village?—A desert?"

Highly excited, Godfrey mounted the hill, keeping his elbows at his chest to restrain the beating of his heart. His panting tired him, but he had not the patience to stop so as to recover himself. Were he to have fallen half fainting on the summit of the cone which shot up about 100 feet above his head, he would not have lost a minute in hastening towards it.

A few minutes more and he would be there. The ascent seemed to him steep enough on his side, an angle perhaps of thirty or thirty-five degrees. He helped himself up with hands and feet; he seized on the tufts of slender herbs on the hill-side, and on a few meagre shrubs, mastics and myrtles, which stretched away up to the top.

A last effort was made! His head rose above the platform of the cone, and then, lying on his stomach, his eyes gazed at the eastern horizon.

It was the sea which formed it. Twenty miles off it united with the line of the sky!

He turned round.

Still sea—west of him, south of him, north of him! The immense ocean surrounding him on all sides!

"An island!"

As he uttered the word Godfrey felt his heart shrink. The thought had not occurred to him that he was on an island. And yet such was the case! The terrestrial chain which should have attached him to the continent was abruptly broken. He felt as though he had been a sleeping man in a drifted boat, who awoke with neither oar nor sail to help him back to shore.

But Godfrey was soon himself again. His part was taken, to accept the situation. If the chances of safety did not come from without, it was for him to contrive them.

He set to work at first then as exactly as possible to ascertain the disposition of this island which his view embraced over its whole length. He estimated that it ought to measure about sixty miles round, being, as far as he could see, about twenty miles long from south to north, and twelve miles wide from east to west.

Its central part was screened by the green depths of forest which extended up to the ridge dominated by the cone, whose slope died away on the shore.

All the rest was prairie, with clumps of trees, or beach with rocks, whose outer ring was capriciously tapered off in the form of capes and promontories. A few creeks cut out the coast, but could only afford refuge for two or three fishing-boats.

The bay at the bottom of which the *Dream* lay shipwrecked was the only one of any size, and that extended over some seven or eight miles. An open roadstead, no vessel would have found it a safe shelter, at least unless the wind was blowing from the east.

But what was this island? To what geographical group did it belong? Did it form part of an archipelago, or was it alone in this portion of the Pacific?

In any case, no other island, large or small, high or low, appeared within the range of vision.

Godfrey rose and gazed round the horizon. Nothing was to be seen along the circular line where sea and sky ran into each other. If, then, there existed to windward or to leeward any island or coast of a continent, it could only be at a considerable distance.

Godfrey called up all his geographical reminiscences, in order to discover what island of the Pacific this could be. In reasoning it out he came to this conclusion.

The *Dream* for seventeen days had steered very nearly southwest. Now with a speed of from 150 to 180 miles every four-and-twenty hours, she ought to have covered nearly fifty degrees. Now it was obvious that she had not crossed the equator.

The situation of the island, or of the group to which it belonged, would therefore have to be looked for in that part of the ocean comprised between the 160th and 170th degrees of west longitude.

In this portion of the Pacific it seemed to Godfrey that the map showed no other archipelago than that of the Sandwich Islands, but outside this archipelago were there not any isolated islands whose names escaped him and which were dotted here and there over the sea up to the coast of the Celestial Empire?

It was not of much consequence. There existed no means of his going in search of another spot on the ocean which might prove more hospitable.

61

"Well," said Godfrey to himself, "if I don't know the name of this island, I'll call it Phina Island, in memory of her I ought never to have left to run about the world, and perhaps the name will bring us some luck."

Godfrey then occupied himself in trying to ascertain if the island was inhabited in the part which he had not yet been able to visit.

From the top of the cone he saw nothing which betrayed the presence of aborigines, neither habitations on the prairie nor houses on the skirt of the trees, not even a fisherman's hut on the shore.

But if the island was deserted, the sea which surrounded it was none the less so, for not a ship showed itself within the limits of what, from the height of the cone, was a considerable circuit.

Godfrey having finished his exploration had now only to get down to the foot of the hill and retake the road through the forest so as to rejoin Tartlet. But before he did so his eyes were attracted by a sort of cluster of trees of huge stature, which rose on the boundary of the prairie towards the north. It was a gigantic group, it exceeded by a head all those which Godfrey had previously seen.

"Perhaps," he said, "it would be better to take up our quarters over there, more especially as if I am not mistaken I can see a stream which should rise in the central chain and flow across the prairie."

This was to be looked into on the morrow.

Towards the south the aspect of the island was slightly different. Forests and prairies rapidly gave place to the yellow carpet of the beach, and in places the shore was bounded with picturesque rocks.

But what was Godfrey's surprise, when he thought he saw a light smoke, which rose in the air beyond this rocky barrier.

"Are there any of our companions?" he exclaimed. "But no, it is not possible! Why should they have got so far from the bay since yesterday, and round so many miles of reef? Is it a village of fishermen, or the encampment of some indigenous tribe?"

Godfrey watched it with the closest attention. Was this gentle vapour which the breeze softly blew towards the west a smoke? Could he be mistaken? Anyhow it quickly vanished, a few minutes afterwards nothing could be seen of it.

It was a false hope.

Godfrey took a last look in its direction, and then seeing nothing, glided down the slope, and again plunged beneath the trees.

An hour later he had traversed the forest and found himself on its skirt.

There Tartlet awaited him with his two-footed and four-footed flock. And how was the obstinate professor occupying himself? In the same way. A bit of wood was in his right hand another piece in his left, and he still continued his efforts to set them alight. He rubbed and rubbed with a constancy worthy of a better fate.

"Well," he shouted as he perceived Godfrey some distance off—"and the telegraph office?"

"It is not open!" answered Godfrey, who dared not yet tell him anything of the situation.

"And the post?"

"It is shut! But let us have something to eat!—I am dying with hunger! We can talk presently."

And this morning Godfrey and his companion had again to content themselves with a too meagre repast of raw eggs and shell-fish.

"Wholesome diet!" repeated Godfrey to Tartlet, who was hardly of that opinion and picked his food with considerable care.

CHAPTER XI

IN WHICH THE QUESTION OF LODGING IS SOLVED AS WELL AS IT COULD BE

The day was already far advanced. Godfrey resolved to defer till the morrow the task of proceeding to a new abode. But to the pressing questions which the professor propounded on the results of his exploration he ended by replying that it was an island, Phina Island, on which they both had been cast, and that they must think of the means of living before dreaming of the means of departing.

"An island!" exclaimed Tartlet.

"Yes! It is an island!"

"Which the sea surrounds?"

"Naturally."

"But what is it?"

"I have told you, Phina Island, and you understand why I gave it that name."

"No, I do not understand!" answered Tartlet, making a grimace; "and I don't see the resemblance! Miss Phina is surrounded by land, not water!"

After this melancholy reflection, he prepared to pass the night with as little discomfort as possible. Godfrey went off to the reef to get a new stock of eggs and mollusks, with which he had to be contented, and then, tired out, he came back to the tree and soon fell asleep, while Tartlet, whose philosophy would not allow him to accept such a state of affairs, gave himself over to the bitterest meditations. On the morrow, the 28th of June, they were both afoot before the cock had interrupted their slumbers.

To begin with, a hasty breakfast, the same as the day before. Only water from a little brook was advantageously replaced by a little milk given by one of the goats.

Ah! worthy Tartlet! Where were the "mint julep," the "port wine sangaree," the "sherry cobbler," the "sherry cocktail," which he hardly drank, but which were served him at all hours in the bars and taverns of San Francisco? How he envied the poultry, the agouties, and the sheep, who cheerfully quenched their thirst without the addition of such saccharine or alcoholic mixtures to their water from the stream! To these animals no fire was necessary to cook their food; roots and herbs and seeds sufficed, and their breakfast was always served to the minute on their tablecloth of green.

"Let us make a start," said Godfrey.

And behold the two on their way, followed by a procession of domestic animals, who refused to be left behind. Godfrey's idea was to explore, in the north of the island, that portion of the coast on which he had noticed the group of gigantic trees in his view from the cone. But to get there he resolved to keep along the shore. The surf might perhaps have cast up some fragment of the wreck. Perhaps they might find on the beach some of their companions in the *Dream* to which they could give Christian burial. As for finding any one of them living, it was hardly to be hoped for, after a lapse of six-and-thirty hours.

The first line of hills was surmounted, and Godfrey and his companion reached the beginning of the reef, which looked as deserted as it had when they had left it. There they renewed their stock of eggs and mollusks, in case they should fail to find even such meagre resources away to the north. Then, following the fringe of sea-weed left by the last tide, they again ascended the dunes, and took a good look round.

Nothing! always nothing!

We must certainly say that if misfortune had made Crusoes of these survivors of the *Dream*, it had shown itself much more rigorous towards them than towards their predecessors, who always had some portion of the vessel left to them, and who, after bringing away crowds of objects of necessity had been able to utilize the timbers of the wreck. Victuals for a considerable period, clothes, tools, weapons, had always been left them with which to satisfy the elementary exigencies of existence. But here there was nothing of all this! In the middle of that dark night the ship had disappeared in the depths of the sea, without leaving on the reefs the slightest traces of its wreck! It had not been possible to save a thing from her—not even a lucifer-match—and to tell the truth, the want of that match was the most serious of all wants.

I know well, good people comfortably installed in your easy-chairs before a comfortable hearth at which is blazing brightly a fire of wood or coals, that you will be apt to say,—

"But nothing was more easy than for them to get a fire! There are a thousand ways of doing that! Two pebbles! A little dry moss! A little burnt rag,"—and how do you burn the rag? "The blade of a knife would do for a steel, or two bits of wood rubbed briskly together in Polynesian fashion!"

Well, try it!

It was about this that Godfrey was thinking as he walked, and this it was that occupied his thoughts more than anything else.

65

Perhaps he too, poking his coke fire and reading his travellers' tales, had thought the same as you good people! But now he had to put matters to the test, and he saw with considerable disquietude the want of a fire, that indispensable element which nothing could replace.

He kept on ahead, then, lost in thought, followed by Tartlet, who by his shouts and gestures, kept together the flock of sheep, agouties, goats, and poultry.

Suddenly his look was attracted by the bright colours of a cluster of small apples which hung from the branches of certain shrubs, growing in hundreds at the foot of the dunes. He immediately recognized them as "manzanillas," which serve as food to the Indians in certain parts of California.

"At last," he exclaimed, "there is something which will be a change from our eggs and mussels."

"What? Do you eat those things?" said Tartlet with his customary grimace.

"You shall soon see!" answered Godfrey.

And he set to work to gather the manzanillas, and eat them greedily.

They were only wild apples, but even their acidity did not prevent them from being agreeable. The professor made little delay in imitating his companion, and did not show himself particularly discontented at the work. Godfrey thought, and with reason, that from these fruits there could be made a fermented liquor which would be preferable to the water.

The march was resumed. Soon the end of the sand dunes died away in a prairie traversed by a small stream. This was the one Godfrey had seen from the top of the cone. The large trees appeared further on, and after a journey of about nine miles the two explorers, tired enough by their four hours' walk, reached them a few minutes after noon.

The site was well worth the trouble of looking at, of visiting, and, doubtless, occupying.

On the edge of a vast prairie, dotted with manzanilla bushes and other shrubs, there rose a score of gigantic trees which could have even borne comparison with the same species in the forests of California. They were arranged in a semi-circle. The carpet of verdure, which stretched at their feet, after bordering the stream for some hundreds of feet, gave place to a long beach, covered with rocks, and shingle, and sea-weed, which ran out into the water in a narrowing point to the north.

These "big trees," as they are commonly called in Western

66

America, belong to the genus *Sequoia*, and are conifers of the fir family. If you ask the English for their distinguishing name, you will be told "Wellingtonias," if you ask the Americans they will reply "Washingtonias." But whether they recall the memory of the phlegmatic victor of Waterloo, or of the illustrious founder of the American Republic, they are the hugest products known of the Californian and Nevadan floras. In certain districts in these states there are entire forests of these trees, such as the groups at Mariposa and Calaveras, some of the trees of which measure from sixty to eighty feet in circumference, and some 300 feet in height. One of them, at the entrance of the Yosemite Valley, is quite 100 feet round. When living—for it is now prostrate—its first branches could have overtopped Strasburg Cathedral, or, in other words, were above eighty feet from the ground.

Besides this tree there are "The Mother of the Forest," "The Beauty of the Forest," "The Hut of the Pioneer," "The Two Sentinels," "General Grant," "Miss Emma," "Miss Mary," "Brigham Young and his Wife," "The Three Graces," "The Bear," &c., &c.; all of them veritable vegetable phenomena. One of the trees has been sawn across at its base, and on it there has been built a ball-room, in which a quadrille of eight or ten couples can be danced with ease.

But the giant of giants, in a forest which is the property of the state, about fifteen miles from Murphy, is "The Father of the Forest," an old sequoia, 4000 years old, which rises 452 feet from the ground, higher than the cross of St. Peter's, at Rome, higher than the great pyramid of Ghizeh, higher than the iron bell-turret which now caps one of the towers of Rouen Cathedral, and which ought to be looked upon as the highest monument in the world.

It was a group of some twenty of these colossi that nature had planted on this point of the island, at the epoch, probably, when Solomon was building that temple at Jerusalem which has never risen from its ruins. The largest was, perhaps, 300 feet high, the smallest nearly 200.

Some of them, hollowed out by age, had enormous arches through their bases, beneath which a troop of horsemen could have ridden with ease.

Godfrey was struck with admiration in the presence of these natural phenomena, as they are not generally found at altitudes of less than from 5000 to 6000 feet above the level of the sea. He even thought that the view alone was worth the journey. Nothing he had seen was comparable to these columns of clear brown, which outlined themselves almost without sensible diminution of their diameters to their lowest fork. The cylindrical trunks rising from 80 to 100 feet above the earth, ramified into such thick branches that they themselves looked like tree-stems of huge dimensions bearing quite a forest in the air.

One of these specimens of *Sequoia gigantea*—one of the biggest in the group—more particularly attracted Godfrey's attention.

Gazing at its base it displayed an opening of from four to five feet in width, and ten feet high, which gave entrance to its interior. The giant's heart had disappeared, the alburnum had been dissipated into soft whitish dust; but if the tree did not depend so much on its powerful roots as on its solid bark, it could still keep its position for centuries.

"In default of a cavern or a grotto," said Godfrey, "here is a ready-made dwelling. A wooden house, a tower, such as there is in no inhabited land. Here we can be sheltered and shut in. Come along, Tartlet! come!"

And the young man, catching hold of his companion, dragged him inside the sequoia.

The base was covered with a bed of vegetable dust, and in diameter could not be less than twenty feet.

As for the height to which its vault extended, the gloom prevented even an estimate. For not a ray of light found its way through the bark wall. Neither cleft nor fault was there through which the wind or rain could come. Our two Crusoes would therein find themselves in a position to brave with impunity the inclemency of the weather. No cave could be firmer, or drier, or compacter. In truth it would have been difficult to have anywhere found a better.

"Eh, Tartlet, what do you think of our natural house?" asked Godfrey.

"Yes, but the chimney?" answered Tartlet.

"Before we talk about the chimney," replied Godfrey, "let us wait till we have got the fire!"

This was only logical.

Godfrey went to reconnoitre the neighbourhood. As we have said, the prairie extended to this enormous mass of sequoias which formed its edge. The small stream meandering through the grassy carpet gave a healthy freshness to its borders, and thereon grew shrubs of different kinds; myrtles, mastic bushes, and among others a quantity of manzanillas, which gave promise of a large crop of their wild apples.

Farther off, on ground that grew gradually higher, were scattered several clumps of trees, made up of oaks and beeches, sycamores and nettle-trees, but trees of great stature as they were, they seemed but simple underwood by the side of the "mammoths," whose huge shadows the sun was throwing even into the sea. Across the prairie lay minor lines of bushes, and vegetable clumps and verdant thickets, which Godfrey resolved to investigate on the following day.

If the site pleased him, it did not displease the domestic animals. Agouties, goats, and sheep had soon taken possession of this domain, which offered them roots to nibble at, and grass to browse on far beyond their needs. As for the fowls they were greedily pecking away at the seeds and worms in the banks of the rivulet. Animal life was already manifesting itself in such goings and comings, such flights and gambols, such bleatings and gruntings and cluckings as had doubtless never been heard of in these parts before.

Then Godfrey returned to the clump of sequoias, and made a more attentive examination of the tree in which he had chosen to take up his abode. It appeared to him that it would be difficult, if not impossible, to climb into the first branches, at least by the exterior; for the trunk presented no protuberances. Inside it the ascent might be easier, if the tree were hollow up to the fork.

In case of danger it would be advisable to seek refuge among the thick boughs borne by the enormous trunk. But this matter could be looked into later on.

When he had finished his inquiries the sun was low on horizon, and it seemed best to put off till to-morrow the preparations for their definitely taking up their abode.

But, after a meal with dessert composed of wild apples, what could they do better than pass the night on a bed of the vegetable dust which covered the ground inside the sequoia?

And this, under the keeping of Providence, was what was done, but not until after Godfrey, in remembrance of his uncle, William W. Kolderup, had given to the giant the name of "Will Tree," just as its prototypes in the forests of California and the neighbouring states bear the names of the great citizens of the American Republic.

CHAPTER XII

WHICH ENDS WITH A THUNDER-BOLT

It must be acknowledged that Godfrey was in a fair way to become a new man in this completely novel position to one so frivolous, so light-minded, and so thoughtless. He had hitherto only had to allow himself to live. Never had care for the morrow disquieted his rest. In the opulent mansion in Montgomery Street, where he slept his ten hours without a break, not the fall of a rose leaf had ever troubled his slumbers.

It was so no longer. On this unknown land he found himself thoroughly shut off from the rest of the world, left entirely to his own resources, obliged to face the necessities of life under conditions in which a man even much more practical might have been in great difficulty. Doubtless when it was found that the *Dream* did not return, a search for him would be made. But what were these two? Less than a needle in a hayrick or a sand-grain on the sea-bottom! The incalculable fortune of Uncle Kolderup could not do everything.

When Godfrey had found his fairly acceptable shelter, his sleep in it was by no means undisturbed. His brain travelled as it had never done before. Ideas of all kinds were associated together: those of the past which he bitterly regretted, those of the present of which he sought the realization, those of the future which disquieted him more than all!

But in these rough trials, the reason and, in consequence, the reasoning which naturally flows from it, were little by little freed from the limbo in which they had hitherto slept. Godfrey was resolved to strive against his ill-luck, and to do all he could to get out of his difficulties. If he escaped, the lesson would certainly not be lost on him for the future.

At daybreak he was astir, with the intention of proceeding to a more complete installation. The question of food, above all that of fire, which was connected with it, occupied the first place; then there were tools or arms to make, clothes to procure, unless they were anxious of soon appearing attired in Polynesian costume.

Tartlet still slumbered. You could not see him in the shadow, but you could hear him. That poor man, spared from the wreck, remained as frivolous at forty-five as his pupil had formerly been. He was a gain in no sense. He even might be considered an incubus, for he had to be cared for in all ways. But he was a companion!

He was worth more in that than the most intelligent dog, although he was probably of less use! He was a creature able to talk—although only at random; to converse—if the matter were never serious; to complain—and this he did most frequently! As it was, Godfrey was able to hear a human voice. That was worth more than the parrot's in Robinson Crusoe! Even with a Tartlet he would not be alone, and nothing was so disheartening as the thought of absolute solitude.

"Crusoe before Friday, Crusoe after Friday; what a difference!" thought he.

However, on this morning, that of June 29th, Godfrey was not sorry to be alone, so as to put into execution his project of exploring the group of sequoias. Perhaps he would be fortunate enough to discover some fruit, some edible root, which he could bring back—to the extreme satisfaction of the professor. And so he left Tartlet to his dreams, and set out.

A light fog still shrouded the shore and the sea, but already it had commenced to lift in the north and east under the influence of the solar rays, which little by little were condensing it. The day promised to be fine. Godfrey, after having cut himself a substantial walking-stick, went for two miles along that part of the beach which he did not know, and whose return formed the outstretched point of Phina Island.

There he made a first meal of shell-fish, mussels, clams, and especially some capital little oysters which he found in great abundance.

"If it comes to the worst," he said to himself, "we need never die of hunger! Here are thousands of dozens of oysters to satisfy the calls of the most imperious stomach! If Tartlet complains, it is because he does not like mollusks! Well, he will have to like them!"

Decidedly, if the oyster did not absolutely replace bread and meat, it furnished an aliment in no whit less nutritive and in a condition capable of being absorbed in large quantities. But as this mollusk is of very easy digestion, it is somewhat dangerous in its use, to say nothing of its abuse.

This breakfast ended, Godfrey again seized his stick, and struck off obliquely towards the south-east, so as to walk up the right bank of the stream. In this direction, he would cross the prairie up to the groups of trees observed the night before beyond the long lines of shrubs and underwood, which he wished to carefully examine.

Godfrey then advanced in this direction for about two miles. He followed the bank of the stream, carpeted with short herbage

71

and smooth as velvet. Flocks of aquatic birds noisily flew round this being, who, new to them, had come to trouble their domain. Fish of many kinds were seen darting about in the limpid waters of the brook, here abouts some four or five yards wide.

It was evident that there would be no difficulty in catching these fish, but how to cook them? Always this insoluble question!

Fortunately, when Godfrey reached the first line of shrubs he recognized two sorts of fruits or roots. One sort had to pass through the fiery trial before being eaten, the other was edible in its natural state. Of these two vegetables the American Indians make constant use.

The first was a shrub of the kind called "camas," which thrives even in lands unfit for culture. With these onion-like roots, should it not be found preferable to treat them as potatoes, there is made a sort of flour very rich and glutinous. But either way, they have to be subjected to a certain cooking, or drying.

The other bush produces a species of bulb of oblong form, bearing the indigenous name of "yamph," and if it possesses less nutritive principles than the camas, it is much the better for one thing,—it can be eaten raw.

Godfrey, highly pleased at his discovery, at once satisfied his hunger on a few of these excellent roots, and not forgetting Tartlet's breakfast, collected a large bundle, and throwing it over his shoulder, retook the road to Will Tree.

That he was well received on his arrival with the crop of yamphs need not be insisted on. The professor greedily regaled himself, and his pupil had to caution him to be moderate.

"Ah!" he said. "We have got some roots to-day. Who knows whether we shall have any to-morrow?"

"Without any doubt," replied Godfrey, "to-morrow and the day after, and always. There is only the trouble of going and fetching them."

"Well, Godfrey, and the camas?"

"Of the camas we will make flour and bread when we have got a fire."

"Fire!" exclaimed the professor, shaking his head. "Fire! And how shall we make it?"

"I don't know yet, but somehow or other we will get at it."

"May Heaven hear you, my dear Godfrey! And when I think that there are so many fellows in this world who have only got to rub a bit of wood on the sole of their boot to get it, it annoys me! No! Never would I have believed that ill-luck would have reduced me to this state! You need not take three steps down Montgomery Street,

72

before you will meet with a gentleman, cigar in mouth, who thinks it a pleasure to give you a light, and here—"

"Here we are not in San Francisco, Tartlet, nor in Montgomery Street, and I think it would be wiser for us not to reckon on the kindness of those we meet!"

"But, why is cooking necessary for bread and meat? Why did not nature make us so that we might live upon nothing?"

"That will come, perhaps!" answered Godfrey with a good-humoured smile.

"Do you think so?"

"I think that our scientists are probably working out the subject."

"Is it possible! And how do they start on their research as to this new mode of alimentation?"

"On this line of reasoning," answered Godfrey, "as the functions of digestion and respiration are connected, the endeavour is to substitute one for the other. Hence the day when chemistry has made the aliments necessary for the food of man capable of assimilation by respiration, the problem will be solved. There is nothing wanted beyond rendering the air nutritious. You will breathe your dinner instead of eating it, that is all!"

"Ah! Is it not a pity that this precious discovery is not yet made!" exclaimed the professor. "How cheerfully would I breathe half a dozen sandwiches and a silverside of beef, just to give me an appetite!"

And Tartlet plunged into a semi-sensuous reverie, in which he beheld succulent atmospheric dinners, and at them unconsciously opened his mouth and breathed his lungs full, oblivious that he had scarcely the wherewithal to feed upon in the ordinary way.

Godfrey roused him from his meditation, and brought him back to the present. He was anxious to proceed to a more complete installation in the interior of Will Tree.

The first thing to do was to clean up their future dwelling-place. It was at the outset necessary to bring out several bushels of that vegetable dust which covered the ground and in which they sank almost up to their knees. Two hours' work hardly sufficed to complete this troublesome task, but at length the chamber was clear of the pulverulent bed, which rose in clouds at the slightest movement.

The ground was hard and firm, as if floored with joists, the large roots of the sequoia ramifying over its surface. It was uneven but solid. Two corners were selected for the beds and of these several bundles of herbage, thoroughly dried in the sun, were to form the materials. As for other furniture, benches, stools, or tables, it was not impossible to make the most indispensable things, for Godfrey had a capital knife, with its saw and gimlet. The companions would have to keep inside during rough weather, and they could eat and work there. Daylight did not fail them, for it streamed through the opening. Later on, if it became necessary to close this aperture for greater safety, Godfrey could try and pierce one or two embrasures in the bark of the sequoia to serve as windows.

As for discovering to what height the opening ran up into the trunk, Godfrey could not do so without a light. All that he could do was to find out with the aid of a pole ten or twelve feet long, held above his head, that he could not touch the top.

The question, however, was not an urgent one. It would be solved eventually.

The day passed in these labours, which were not ended at sunset. Godfrey and Tartlet, tired as they were, found their novel bed-clothes formed of the dried herbage, of which they had an ample supply, most excellent; but they had to drive away the poultry who would willingly have roosted in the interior of Will Tree. Then occurred to Godfrey the idea of constructing a poultry-house in some other sequoia, as, to keep them out of the common room, he was building up a hurdle of brushwood. Fortunately neither the sheep nor the agouties, nor the goats experienced the like temptation. These animals remained quietly outside, and had no fancy to get through the insufficient barrier.

The following days were employed in different jobs, in fitting up the house or bringing in food; eggs and shell-fish were collected, yamph roots and manzanilla apples were brought in, and oysters, for which each morning they went to the bank or the shore. All this took time, and the hours passed away quickly.

The "dinner things" consisted now of large bivalve shells, which served for dishes or plates. It is true that for the kind of food to which the hosts of Will Tree were reduced, others were not needed.

There was also the washing of the linen in the clear water of the stream, which occupied the leisure of Tartlet. It was to him that this task fell; but he only had to see to the two shirts, two handkerchiefs, and two pairs of socks, which composed the entire wardrobe of both.

While this operation was in progress, Godfrey and Tartlet had to wear only waistcoat and trousers, but in the blazing sun of that latitude the clothes quickly dried. And so matters went on without either rain or wind till July 3rd. Already they had begun to be fairly comfortable in their new home, considering the condition in which they had been cast on the island.

However, it was advisable not to neglect the chances of safety which might come from without. Each day Godfrey examined the whole sector of sea which extended from the east to the north-west beyond the promontory.

This part of the Pacific was always deserted. Not a vessel, not a fishing-boat, not a ribbon of smoke detaching itself from the horizon, proclaimed the passage of a steamer. It seemed that Phina Island was situated out of the way of all the itineraries of commerce. All they could do was to wait, trusting in the Almighty who never abandons the weak.

Meanwhile, when their immediate necessities allowed them leisure, Godfrey, incited by Tartlet, returned to that important and vexed question of the fire.

He tried at first to replace amadou, which he so unfortunately lacked, by another and analogous material. It was possible that some of the varieties of mushrooms which grew in the crevices of the old trees, after having been subjected to prolonged drying, might be transformed into a combustible substance.

Many of these mushrooms were collected and exposed to the direct action of the sun, until they were reduced to powder. Then with the back of his knife, Godfrey endeavoured to strike some sparks off with a flint, so that they might fall on this substance. It was useless. The spongy stuff would not catch fire. Godfrey then tried to use that fine vegetable dust, dried during so many centuries, which he had found in the interior of Will Tree. The result was equally discouraging.

In desperation he then, by means of his knife and flint, strove to secure the ignition of a sort of sponge which grew under the rocks. He fared no better. The particle of steel, lighted by the impact of the silex, fell on to the substance, but went out immediately. Godfrey and Tartlet were in despair. To do without fire was impossible. Of their fruits and mollusks they were getting tired, and their stomachs began to revolt at such food. They eyed, the professor especially, the sheep, agouties, and fowls which went and came round Will Tree. The pangs of hunger seized them as they gazed. With their eyes they ate the living meat!

No! It could not go on like this!

But an unexpected circumstance, a providential one if you will, came to their aid.

In the night of the 3rd of July the weather, which had been on the change for a day or so, grew stormy, after an oppressive heat which the sea-breeze had been powerless to temper.

Godfrey and Tartlet at about one o'clock in the morning were awakened by heavy claps of thunder, and most vivid flashes of lightning. It did not rain as yet, but it soon promised to do so, and then regular cataracts would be precipitated from the cloudy zone, owing to the rapid condensation of the vapour.

Godfrey got up and went out so as to observe the state of the sky.

There seemed quite a conflagration above the domes of the giant trees and the foliage appeared on fire against the sky, like the fine network of a Chinese shadow.

Suddenly, in the midst of the general uproar, a vivid flash illuminated the atmosphere. The thunder-clap followed immediately, and Will Tree was permeated from top to bottom with the electric force.

Godfrey, staggered by the return shock, stood in the midst of a rain of fire which showered around him. The lightning had ignited the dry branches above him. They were incandescent particles of carbon which crackled at his feet.

Godfrey with a shout awoke his companion.

"Fire! Fire!"

"Fire!" answered Tartlet. "Blessed be Heaven which sends it to us!"

Instantly they possessed themselves of the flaming twigs, of which some still burned, while others had been consumed in the flames. Hurriedly, at the same time, did they heap together a quantity of dead wood such as was never wanting at the foot of the sequoia, whose trunk had not been touched by the lightning.

Then they returned into their gloomy habitation as the rain, pouring down in sheets, extinguished the fire which threatened to devour the upper branches of Will Tree.

CHAPTER XIII

IN WHICH GODFREY AGAIN SEES A SLIGHT SMOKE OVER ANOTHER PART OF THE ISLAND

That was a storm which came just when it was wanted! Godfrey and Tartlet had not, like Prometheus, to venture into space to bring down the celestial fire! "It was," said Tartlet, "as if the sky had been obliging enough to send it down to them on a lightning flash."

With them now remained the task of keeping it!

"No! we must not let it go out!" Godfrey had said.

"Not until the wood fails us to feed it!" had responded Tartlet, whose satisfaction showed itself in little cries of joy.

"Yes! but who will keep it in?"

"I! I will! I will watch it day and night, if necessary," replied Tartlet, brandishing a flaming bough.

And he did so till the sun rose.

Dry wood, as we have said, abounded beneath the sequoias. Until the dawn Godfrey and the professor, after heaping up a considerable stock, did not spare to feed the fire. By the foot of one of the large trees in a narrow space between the roots the flames leapt up, crackling clearly and joyously. Tartlet exhausted his lungs blowing away at it, although his doing so was perfectly useless. In this performance he assumed the most characteristic attitudes in following the greyish smoke whose wreaths were lost in the foliage above.

But it was not that they might admire it that they had so longingly asked for this indispensable fire, not to warm themselves at it. It was destined for a much more interesting use. There was to be an end of their miserable meals of raw mollusks and yamph roots, whose nutritive elements boiling water and simple cooking in the ashes had never developed. It was in this way that Godfrey and Tartlet employed it during the morning.

"We could eat a fowl or two!" exclaimed Tartlet, whose jaws moved in anticipation. "Not to mention an agouti ham, a leg of mutton, a quarter of goat, some of the game on the prairie, without counting two or three freshwater fish and a sea fish or so."

"Not so fast," answered Godfrey, whom the declaration of this modest bill of fare had put in good humour. "We need not risk indigestion to satisfy a fast! We must look after our reserves,

77

Tartlet! Take a couple of fowls—one apiece—and if we want bread, I hope that our camsa roots can be so prepared as to replace it with advantage!" This cost the lives of two innocent hens, who, plucked, trussed, and dressed by the professor, were stuck on a stick, and soon roasted before the crackling flames.

Meanwhile, Godfrey was getting the camas roots in a state to figure creditably at the first genuine breakfast on Phina Island. To render them edible it was only necessary to follow the Indian method, which the Californians were well acquainted with.

This was what Godfrey did.

A few flat stones selected from the beach were thrown in the fire so as to get intensely hot. Tartlet seemed to think it a great shame to use such a good fire "to cook stones with," but as it did not hinder the preparation of his fowls in any way he had no other complaint to make.

While the stones were getting warm Godfrey selected a piece of ground about a yard square from which he tore up the grass; then with his hands armed with large scallop shells he dug the soil to the depth of about ten inches. That done he laid at the bottom of the cavity a fire of dry wood, which he so arranged as to communicate to the earth heaped up at its bottom some considerable heat.

When all the wood had been consumed and the cinders taken away, the camas roots, previously cleaned and scraped, were strewn in the hole, a thin layer of sods thrown over them and the glowing stones placed on the top, so as to serve as the basis of a new fire which was lighted on their surface.

In fact, it was a kind of oven which had been prepared; and in a very short time—about half an hour or so—the operation was at an end.

Beneath the double layer of stones and sods lay the roots cooked by this violent heating. On crushing them there was obtainable a flour well fitted for making into bread, but, even eaten as they were, they proved much like potatoes of highly nutritive quality.

It was thus that this time the roots were served and we leave our readers to imagine what a breakfast our two friends made on the chickens which they devoured to the very bones, and on the excellent camas roots, of which they had no need to be sparing. The field was not far off where they grew in abundance. They could be picked up in hundreds by simply stooping down for them.

The repast over, Godfrey set to work to prepare some of the flour, which keeps for any length of time, and which could be transformed into bread for their daily wants.

The day was passed in different occupations. The fire was kept up with great care. Particularly was the fuel heaped on for the night; and Tartlet, nevertheless, arose on many occasions to sweep the ashes together and provoke a more active combustion. Having done this, he would go to bed again, to get up as soon as the fire burnt low, and thus he occupied himself till the day broke. The night passed without incident, the cracklings of the fire and the crow of the cock awoke Godfrey and his companion, who had ended his performances by falling off to sleep.

At first Godfrey was surprised at feeling a current of air coming down from above in the interior of Will Tree. He was thus led to think that the sequoia was hollow up to the junction of the lower branches where there was an opening which they would have to stop up if they wished to be snug and sheltered.

"But it is very singular!" said Godfrey to himself.

"How was it that during the preceding nights I did not feel this current of air? Could it have been the lightning?"

And to get an answer to this question, the idea occurred to him to examine the trunk of the sequoia from the out side.

When he had done so, he understood what had happened during the storm.

The track of the lightning was visible on the tree, which had had a long strip of its bark torn off from the fork down to the roots.

Had the electric spark found its way into the interior of the sequoia in place of keeping to the outside, Godfrey and his companion would have been struck. Most decidedly they had had a narrow escape.

"It is not a good thing to take refuge under trees during a storm," said Godfrey. "That is all very well for people who can do otherwise. But what way have we to avoid the danger who live inside the tree? We must see!"

Then examining the sequoia from the point where the long lightning trace began—"It is evident," said he, "that where the flash struck the tree has been cracked. But since the air penetrates by this orifice the tree must be hollow along its whole length and only lives in its bark? Now that is what I ought to see about!"

And Godfrey went to look for a resinous piece of wood that might do for a torch.

A bundle of pine twigs furnished him with the torch he needed, as from them exuded a resin which, once inflamed, gave forth a brilliant light.

Godfrey then entered the cavity which served him for his house. To darkness immediately succeeded light, and it was easy to see the state of the interior of Will Tree. A sort of vault of irregular formation stretched across in a ceiling some fifteen feet above the ground. Lifting his torch Godfrey distinctly saw that into this there opened a narrow passage whose further development was lost in the shadow. The tree was evidently hollow throughout its length; but perhaps some portion of the alburnum still remained intact. In that case, by the help of the protuberances it would be possible if not easy to get up to the fork.

Godfrey, who was thinking of the future, resolved to know without delay if this were so.

He had two ends in view; one, to securely close the opening by which the rain and wind found admission, and so render Will Tree almost habitable; the other, to see if in case of danger, or an attack from animals or savages, the upper branches of the tree would not afford a convenient refuge.

He could but try. If he encountered any insurmountable obstacle in the narrow passage, Godfrey could be got down again.

After firmly sticking his torch between two of the roots below, behold him then commencing to raise himself on to the first interior knots of the bark. He was lithe, strong, and accustomed to gymnastics like all young Americans. It was only sport to him. Soon he had reached in this uneven tube a part much narrower, in which, with the aid of his back and knees, he could work his way upwards like a chimney-sweep. All he feared was that the hole would not continue large enough for him to get up.

However, he kept on, and each time he reached a projection he would stop and take breath.

Three minutes after leaving the ground, Godfrey had mounted about sixty feet, and consequently could only have about twenty feet further to go.

In fact, he already felt the air blowing more strongly on his face. He inhaled it greedily, for the atmosphere inside the sequoia was not, strictly speaking, particularly fresh.

After resting for a minute, and shaking off the fine dust which he had rubbed on to him off the wall, Godfrey started again up the long tunnel, which gradually narrowed.

But at this moment his attention was attracted by a peculiar noise, which appeared to him somewhat suspicious. There was a sound as of scratching, up the tree. Almost immediately a sort of hissing was heard.

Godfrey stopped.

"What is that?" he asked. "Some animal taken refuge in the

80

sequoia? Was it a snake? No! We have not yet seen one on the island! Perhaps it is a bird that wants to get out!"

Godfrey was not mistaken; and as he continued to mount, a cawing, followed by a rapid flapping of wings, showed him that it was some bird ensconced in the tree whose sleep he was doubtless disturbing.

Many a "frrr-frrr!" which he gave out with the whole power of his lungs, soon determined the intruder to clear off.

It proved to be a kind of jackdaw, of huge stature, which scuttled out of the opening, and disappeared into the summit of Will Tree.

A few seconds afterwards, Godfrey's head appeared through the same opening, and he soon found himself quite at his ease, installed on a fork of the tree where the lower branches gave off, at about eighty feet from the ground.

There, as has been said, the enormous stem of the sequoia supported quite a forest. The capricious network of its upper boughs presented the aspect of a wood crowded with trees, which no gap rendered passable.

However, Godfrey managed, not without difficulty, to get along from one branch to another, so as to gain little by little the upper story of this vegetable phenomenon.

A number of birds with many a cry flew off at his approach, and hastened to take refuge in the neighbouring members of the group, above which Will Tree towered by more than a head.

Godfrey continued to climb as well as he could, and did not stop until the ends of the higher branches began to bend beneath his weight.

A huge horizon of water surrounded Phina Island, which lay unrolled like a relief-map at his feet. Greedily his eyes examined that portion of the sea. It was still deserted. He had to conclude once more, that the island lay away from the trade routes of the Pacific.

Godfrey uttered a heavy sigh; then his look fell on the narrow domain on which fate had condemned him to live, doubtless for long, perhaps for ever.

But what was his surprise when he saw, this time away to the north, a smoke similar to that which he had already thought he had seen in the south. He watched it with the keenest attention.

A very light vapour, calm and pure, greyish blue at its tip, rose straight in the air.

"No! I am not mistaken!" exclaimed Godfrey. "There is a

smoke, and therefore a fire which produces it! And that fire could not have been lighted except by—By whom?"

Godfrey then with extreme precision took the bearings of the spot in question.

The smoke was rising in the north-east of the island, amid the high rocks which bordered the beach. There was no mistake about that. It was less than five miles from Will Tree. Striking straight to the north-east across the prairie, and then following the shore, he could not fail to find the rocks above which the vapour rose.

With beating heart Godfrey made his way down the scaffolding of branches until he reached the fork. There he stopped an instant to clear off the moss and leaves which clung to him, and that done he slid down the opening, which he enlarged as much as possible, and rapidly gained the ground. A word to Tartlet not to be uneasy at his absence, and Godfrey hastened off in the north-easterly direction so as to reach the shore.

It was a two hours' walk across the verdant prairie, through clumps of scattered trees, or hedges of spiny shrubs, and then along the beach. At length the last chain of rocks was reached.

But the smoke which Godfrey had seen from the top of the tree he searched for in vain when he had reached the ground. As he had taken the bearings of the spot with great care, he came towards it without any mistake.

There Godfrey began his search. He carefully explored every nook and corner of this part of the shore. He called. No one answered to his shout. No human being appeared on the beach. Not a rock gave him a trace of a newly lighted fire—nor of a fire now extinct, which could have been fed by sea herbs and dry algæ thrown up by the tide.

"But it is impossible that I should have been mistaken!" repeated Godfrey to himself. "I am sure it was smoke that I saw! And besides!—"

As Godfrey could not admit that he had been the dupe of a delusion, he began to think that there must exist some well of heated water, or kind of intermittent geyser, which he could not exactly find, but which had given forth the vapour.

There was nothing to show that in the island there were not many of such natural wells, and the apparition of the column of smoke could be easily explained by so simple a geological phenomenon.

Godfrey left the shore and returned towards Will Tree, observing the country as he went along a little more carefully than he had done as he came. A few ruminants showed themselves, amongst others some wapiti, but they dashed past with such speed that it was impossible to get near them.

In about four hours Godfrey got back. Just before he reached the tree he heard the shrill "twang! squeak!" of the kit, and soon found himself face to face with Professor Tartlet, who, in the attitude of a vestal, was watching the sacred fire confided to his keeping.

CHAPTER XIV

WHEREIN GODFREY FINDS SOME WRECKAGE, TO WHICH HE AND HIS COMPANION GIVE A HEARTY WELCOME

To put up with what you cannot avoid is a philosophical principle, that may not perhaps lead you to the accomplishment of great deeds, but is assuredly eminently practical. On this principle Godfrey had resolved to act for the future. If he had to live in this island, the wisest thing for him to do was to live there as comfortably as possible until an opportunity offered for him to leave it.

And so, without delay, he set to work to get the interior of Will Tree into some order. Cleanliness was of the first importance. The beds of dried grass were frequently renewed. The plates and dishes were only scallop shells, it is true, but no American kitchen could show cleaner ones. It should be said to his praise that Professor Tartlet was a capital washer. With the help of his knife Godfrey, by flattening out a large piece of bark, and sticking four uprights into the ground, had contrived a table in the middle of the room. Some large stumps served for stools. The comrades were no longer reduced to eating on their knees, when the weather prevented their dining in the open air.

There was still the question of clothing, which was of great interest to them, and they did the best they could. In that climate, and under that latitude, there was no reason why they should not go about half naked; but, at length, trousers, waistcoat, and linen shirt were all worn out. How could they replace them? Were the sheep and the goats to provide them with skins for clothing, after furnishing them with flesh for food? It looked like it. Meanwhile, Godfrey had the few garments he possessed frequently washed. It was on Tartlet, transformed into a laundress, that this task fell, and he acquitted himself of it to the general satisfaction.

Godfrey busied himself specially in providing food, and in arranging matters generally. He was, in fact, the caterer. Collecting the edible roots and the manzanilla fruit occupied him some hours every day; and so did fishing with plaited rushes, sometimes in the waters of the stream, and sometimes in the hollows of the rocks on the beach when the tide had gone out. The means were primitive, no doubt, but from time to time a fine crustacean or a succulent fish figured on the table of Will Tree, to say nothing of the mollusks, which were easily caught by hand.

But we must confess that the pot—of all the pieces in the battery of the cook undoubtedly the most essential—the simple iron pot, was wanting. Its absence could not but be deeply felt. Godfrey knew not how to replace the vulgar pipkin, whose use is universal. No hash, no stew, no boiled meat, no fish, nothing but roasts and grills. No soup appeared at the beginning of a meal. Constantly and bitterly did Tartlet complain—but how to satisfy the poor man?

Godfrey was busied with other cares. In visiting the different trees of the group he had found a second sequoia of great height, of which the lower part, hollowed out by the weather, was very rugged and uneven.

Here he devised his poultry-house, and in it the fowls took up their abode. The hens soon became accustomed to their home, and settled themselves to set on eggs placed in the dried grass, and chickens began to multiply. Every evening the broods were driven in and shut up, so as to keep them from birds of prey, who, aloft in the branches, watched their easy victims, and would, if they could, have ended by destroying them.

As for the agoutis, the sheep, and the goats, it would have been useless then to have looked out a stable or a shelter for them. When the bad weather came, there would be time enough to see to that. Meanwhile they prospered on the luxuriant pasturage of the prairie, with its abundance of sainfoin and edible roots, of which the porcine representatives showed genuine appreciation. A few kids had been dropped since the arrival in the island, and as much milk as possible was left to the goats with which to nourish their little ones.

From all this it resulted that the surroundings of Will Tree were quite lively. The well-fed domestic animals came during the warm hours of the day to find there a refuge from the heat of the sun. No fear was there of their wandering abroad, or of their falling a prey to wild beasts, of which Phina Island seemed to contain not a single specimen.

And so things went on, with a present fairly comfortable perhaps, but a future very disquieting, when an unexpected incident occurred which bettered the position considerably.

It was on the 29th of July.

Godfrey was strolling in the morning along that part of the shore which formed the beach of the large bight to which he had given the name of Dream Bay. He was exploring it to see if it was as rich in shell-fish as the coast on the north. Perhaps he still hoped that he might yet come across some of the wreck, of which it seemed to him so strange that the tide had as yet brought in not a single fragment.

On this occasion he had advanced to the northern point which terminated in a sandy spit, when his attention was attracted by a rock of curious shape, rising near the last group of algæ and sea-weeds.

A strange presentiment made him hasten his steps. What was his surprise, and his joy, when he saw that what he had taken for a rock was a box, half buried in the sand.

Was it one of the packages of the *Dream*? Had it been here ever since the wreck? Was it not rather all that remained of another and more recent catastrophe? It was difficult to say. In any case no matter whence it came or what it held, the box was a valuable prize.

Godfrey examined it outwardly. There was no trace of an address not even a name, not even one of those huge initials cut out of thin sheet metal which ornament the boxes of the Americans. Perhaps he would find inside it some paper which would indicate the origin, or nationality, or name of the proprietor? Any how it was apparently hermetically sealed, and there was hope that its contents had not been spoiled by their sojourn in the sea-water. It was a very strong wooden box, covered with thick leather, with copper corner plates at the angles, and large straps all over it.

Impatient as he was to view the contents of the box, Godfrey did not think of damaging it, but of opening it after destroying the lock; as to transporting it from the bottom of Dream Bay to Will Tree, its weight forbade it, and he never gave that a thought.

"Well," said Godfrey to himself, "we must empty it where it is, and make as many journeys as may be necessary to take away all that is inside."

It was about four miles from the end of the promontory to the group of sequoias. It would therefore take some time to do this, and occasion considerable fatigue. Time did not press, however. As for the fatigue, it was hardly worth thinking about.

What did the box contain? Before returning to Will Tree, Godfrey had a try at opening it.

He began by unbuckling the straps, and once they were off he very carefully lifted the leather shield which protected the lock. But how was he to force it?

It was a difficult job. Godfrey had no lever with which to bring his strength to bear. He had to guard against the risk of breaking his knife, and so he looked about for a heavy stone with which he could start the staple.

The beach was strewn with lumps of hard silex in every form which could do for a hammer.

Godfrey picked out one as thick as his wrist, and with it he gave a tremendous whack on the plate of copper.

To his extreme surprise the bolt shot through the staple immediately gave way.

Either the staple was broken by the blow, or the lock was not turned.

Godfrey's heart beat high as he stooped to lift up the box lid.

It rose unchecked, and in truth had Godfrey had to get it to pieces he would not have done so without trouble. The trunk was a regular strong-box. The interior was lined with sheet zinc, so that the sea-water had failed to penetrate. The objects it contained, however delicate they might be, would be found in a perfect state of preservation.

And what objects! As he took them out Godfrey could not restrain exclamations of joy! Most assuredly the box must have belonged to some highly practical traveller, who had reckoned on getting into a country where he would have to trust to his own resources.

In the first place there was linen—shirts, table-cloths, sheets, counterpanes; then clothes—woollen jerseys, woollen socks, cotton socks, cloth trousers, velveteen trousers, knitted waistcoats, waistcoats of good heavy stuffs; then two pairs of strong boots, and hunting-shoes and felt hats.

Then came a few kitchen and toilet utensils; and an iron pot—the famous pot which was wanted so badly—a kettle, a coffee-pot, a tea-pot, some spoons, some forks, some knives, a looking-glass, and brushes of all kinds, and, what was by no means to be despised, three cans, containing about fifteen pints of brandy and tafia, and several pounds of tea and coffee.

Then, in the third place, came some tools—an auger, a gimlet, a handsaw, an assortment of nails and brads, a spade, a shovel, a pickaxe, a hatchet, an adze, &c., &c.

In the fourth place, there were some weapons, two hunting-knives in their leather sheaths, a carbine and two muskets, three six-shooter revolvers, a dozen pounds of powder, many thousand caps, and an important stock of lead and bullets, all the arms seeming to be of English make. There was also a small medicine-chest, a telescope, a compass, and a chronometer. There were also a few English books, several quires of blank paper, pencils, pens, and ink, an almanac, a Bible with a New York imprint, and a "Complete Cook's Manual."

Verily this is an inventory of what under the circumstances was an inestimable prize.

Godfrey could not contain himself for joy. Had he expressly ordered the trousseau for the use of shipwrecked folks in difficulties, he could not have made it more complete.

Abundant thanks were due for it to Providence. And Providence had the thanks, and from an overflowing heart.

Godfrey indulged himself in the pleasure of spreading out all his treasure on the beach. Every object was looked over, but not a scrap of paper was there in the box to indicate to whom it belonged, or the ship on which it had been embarked.

Around, the sea showed no signs of a recent wreck.

Nothing was there on the rocks, nothing on the sands. The box must have been brought in by the flood, after being afloat for perhaps many days. In fact, its size in proportion to its weight had assured for it sufficient buoyancy.

The two inhabitants of Phina Island would for some time be kept provided in a large measure with the material wants of life,— tools, arms, instruments, utensils, clothes—due to the luckiest of chances.

Godfrey did not dream of taking all the things to Will Tree at once. Their transport would necessitate several journeys but he would have to make haste for fear of bad weather.

Godfrey then put back most of the things in the box. A gun, a revolver, a certain quantity of powder and lead, a hunting-knife, the telescope, and the iron pot, he took as his first load.

The box was carefully closed and strapped up, and with a rapid step Godfrey strode back along the shore.

Ah! What a reception he had from Tartlet, an hour later! And the delight of the Professor when his pupil ran over the list of their new riches! The pot—that pot above everything—threw him into transports of joy, culminating in a series of "hornpipes" and "cellar-flaps," wound up by a triumphant "six-eight breakdown."

It was only noon as yet. Godfrey wished after the meal to get back at once to Dream Bay. He would never rest until the whole was in safety at Will Tree.

Tartlet made no objection, and declared himself ready to start. It was no longer necessary to watch the fire. With the powder they could always get a light. But the Professor was desirous that during their absence the soup which he was thinking about might be kept gently on the simmer. The wonderful pot was soon filled with water from the stream, a whole quarter of a goat was thrown in, accompanied by a dozen yamph roots, to take the place of vegetables, and then a pinch or two of salt found in the crevices of the rocks gave seasoning to the mixture.

"It must skim itself," exclaimed Tartlet, who seemed highly satisfied at his performance.

And off they started for Dream Bay by the shortest road. The box had not been disturbed. Godfrey opened it with care. Amid a storm of admiring exclamations from Tartlet, he began to pick out the things.

In this first journey Godfrey and his companion, transformed into beasts of burden, carried away to Will Tree the arms, the ammunition, and a part of the wearing apparel.

Then they rested from their fatigue beside the table, on which there smoked the stewed agouti, which they pronounced most excellent. As for the meat, to listen to the Professor it would have been difficult even to imagine anything more exquisite! Oh! the marvellous effect of privation!

On the 30th, the next day, Godfrey and Tartlet set forth at dawn, and in three other journeys succeeded in emptying and carrying away all that the box contained. Before the evening, tools, weapons, instruments, utensils, were all brought, arranged, and stowed away in Will Tree.

On the 1st of August, the box itself, dragged along the beach not without difficulty, found a place in the tree, and was transformed into a linen-closet.

Tartlet, with the fickleness of his mind, now looked upon the future through none but rosy glasses. We can hardly feel astonished then that on this day, with his kit in his hand, he went out to find his pupil, and said to him in all seriousness, as if he were in the drawing-room of Kolderup's mansion,—

"Well, Godfrey, my boy, don't you think it is time to resume our dancing lessons?"

CHAPTER XV

IN WHICH THERE HAPPENS WHAT HAPPENS AT LEAST ONCE IN THE LIFE OF EVERY CRUSOE, REAL OR IMAGINARY

And now the future looked less gloomy. But if Tartlet saw in the possession of the instruments, the tools, and the weapons only the means of making their life of isolation a little more agreeable, Godfrey was already thinking of how to escape from Phina Island. Could he not now construct a vessel strong enough to enable them to reach if not some neighbouring land, at least some ship passing within sight of the island?

Meanwhile the weeks which followed were principally spent in carrying out not these ideas, but those of Tartlet. The wardrobe at Will Tree was now replenished, but it was decided to use it with all the discretion which the uncertainty of the future required. Never to wear any of the clothes unless necessity compelled him to do so, was the rule to which the professor was forced to submit.

"What is the good of that?" grumbled he. "It is a great deal too stingy, my dear Godfrey! Are we savages, that we should go about half naked?"

"I beg your pardon, Tartlet," replied Godfrey; "we are savages, and nothing else."

"As you please; but you will see that we shall leave the island before we have worn the clothes!"

"I know nothing about it, Tartlet, and it is better to have than to want."

"But on Sunday now, surely on Sunday, we might dress up a little?"

"Very well, on Sundays then, and perhaps on public holidays," answered Godfrey, who did not wish to anger his frivolous companion; "but as to day is Monday we shall have to wait a whole week before we come out in our best."

We need hardly mention that from the moment he arrived on the island Godfrey had not omitted to mark each day as it passed. By the aid of the calendar he found in the box he was able to verify that the day was really Monday.

Each performed his daily task according to his ability. It was no longer necessary for them to keep watch by day and night over a fire which they had now the means of relighting.

Tartlet therefore abandoned, not without regret, a task which suited him so well. Henceforwards he took charge of the provisioning with yamph and camas roots—of that in short which formed the daily bread of the establishment, so that the professor went every day and collected them, up to the lines of shrubs with which the prairie was bordered behind Will Tree. It was one or two miles to walk, but he accustomed himself to it. Between whiles he occupied his time in collecting oysters or other mollusks, of which they consumed a great quantity.

Godfrey reserved for himself the care of the domestic animals and the poultry. The butchering trade was hardly to his taste, but he soon overcame his repugnance. Thanks to him, boiled meats appeared frequently on the table, followed by an occasional joint of roast meat to afford a sufficiently varied bill of fare. Game abounded in the woods of Phina Island, and Godfrey proposed to begin his shooting when other more pressing cares allowed him time. He thought of making good use of the guns, powder, and bullets in his arsenal, but he in the first place wished to complete his preparations. His tools enabled him to make several benches inside and outside Will Tree. The stools were cut out roughly with the axe, the table made a little less roughly became more worthy of the dishes and dinner things with which Professor Tartlet adorned it. The beds were arranged in wooden boxes and their litter of dry grass assumed a more inviting aspect. If mattresses and palliasses were still wanting, counterpanes at least were not. The various cooking utensils stood no longer on the ground, but had their places on planks fixed along the walls. Stores, linen, and clothes were carefully put away in cavities hollowed out in the bark of the sequoia. From strong pegs were suspended the arms and instruments, forming quite a trophy on the walls.

Godfrey was also desirous of putting a door to the house, so that the other living creatures—the domestic animals—should not come during the night and trouble their sleep. As he could not cut out boards with his only saw, the handsaw, he used large and thick pieces of bark, which he got off very easily. With these he made a door sufficiently massive to close the opening into Will Tree, at the same time he made two little windows, one opposite to the other, so as to let light and air into the room. Shutters allowed him to close them at night, but from the morning to the evening it was no longer necessary to take refuge in flaring resinous torches which filled the dwelling with smoke. What Godfrey would think of to yield them light during the long nights of winter he had as yet no idea. He might take to making candles with the mutton fat, or he might be contented with resinous torches more carefully prepared. We shall see.

Another of his anxieties was how to construct a chimney in Will Tree. While the fine weather lasted, the fire outside among the roots of the sequoia sufficed for all the wants of the kitchen, but when the bad weather came and the rain fell in torrents, and they would have to battle with the cold, whose extreme rigour during a certain time they reasonably feared, they would have to have a fire inside their house, and the smoke from it must have some vent. This important question therefore had to be settled.

One very useful work which Godfrey undertook was to put both banks of the river in communication with each other on the skirt of the sequoia-trees.

He managed, after some difficulty, to drive a few stakes into the river-bed, and on them he fixed a staging of planks, which served for a bridge. They could thus get away to the northern shore without crossing the ford, which led them a couple of miles out of their road.

But if Godfrey took all these precautions so as to make existence a little more possible on this lone isle of the Pacific, in case he and his companion were destined to live on it for some time, or perhaps live on it for ever, he had no intention of neglecting in any way the chances of rescue.

Phina Island was not on the routes taken by the ships—that was only too evident. It offered no port of call, nor means of revictualling. There was nothing to encourage ships to take notice of it. At the same time it was not impossible that a war-ship or a merchant-vessel might come in sight. It was advisable therefore to find some way of attracting attention, and showing that the island was inhabited.

With this object Godfrey erected a flagstaff at the end of the cape which ran out to the north, and for a flag he sacrificed a piece of one of the cloths found in the trunk. As he thought that the white colour would only be visible in a strong light, he tried to stain his flag with the berries of a sort of shrub which grew at the foot of the dunes. He obtained a very vivid red, which he could not make indelible owing to his having no mordant, but he could easily re-dye the cloth when the wind or rain had faded it.

These varied employments occupied him up to the 15th of August. For many weeks the sky had been constantly clear, with the exception of two or three storms of extreme violence which had brought down a large quantity of water, to be greedily drunk in by the soil.

About this time Godfrey began his shooting expeditions. But if he was skilful enough in the use of the gun, he could not reckon on Tartlet, who had yet to fire his first shot.

Many days of the week did Godfrey devote to the pursuit of fur and feather, which, without being abundant, were yet plentiful enough for the requirements of Will Tree.

A few partridges, some of the red-legged variety, and a few snipes, came as a welcome variation of the bill of fare. Two or three antelopes fell to the prowess of the young stalker; and although he had had nothing to do with their capture, the professor gave them a no less welcome than he did when they appeared as haunches and cutlets.

But while he was out shooting, Godfrey did not forget to take a more complete survey of the island. He penetrated the depths of the dense forests which occupied the central districts. He ascended the river to its source. He again mounted the summit of the cone, and redescended by the talus on the eastern shore, which he had not, up to then, visited.

"After all these explorations," repeated Godfrey to himself, "there can be no doubt that Phina Island has no dangerous animals, neither wild beasts, snakes, nor saurians! I have not caught sight of one! Assuredly if there had been any, the report of the gun would have woke them up! It is fortunate, indeed. If it were to become necessary to fortify Will Tree against their attacks, I do not know how we should get on!"

Then passing on to quite a natural deduction—

"It must also be concluded," continued he, "that the island is not inhabited at all. Either natives or people shipwrecked here would have appeared before now at the sound of the gun! There is, however, that inexplicable smoke which I twice thought I saw."

The fact is, that Godfrey had never been able to trace any fire. As for the hot water springs to which he attributed the origin of the vapour he had noticed, Phina Island being in no way volcanic did not appear to contain any, and he had to content himself with thinking that he had twice been the victim of an illusion.

Besides, this apparition of the smoke or the vapour was not repeated. When Godfrey the second time ascended the central cone, as also when he again climbed up into Will Tree, he saw nothing to attract his attention. He ended by forgetting the circumstance altogether.

Many weeks passed in different occupations about the tree, and many shooting excursions were undertaken. With every day their mode of life improved.

Every Sunday, as had been agreed, Tartlet donned his best clothes. On that day he did nothing but walk about under the big trees, and indulge in an occasional tune on the kit. Many were the glissades he performed, giving lessons to himself, as his pupil had positively refused to continue his course.

"What is the good of it?" was Godfrey's answer to the entreaties of the professor. "Can you imagine Robinson Crusoe taking lessons in dancing and deportment?"

"And why not?" asked Tartlet seriously. "Why should Robinson Crusoe dispense with deportment? Not for the good of others, but of himself, he should acquire refined manners."

To which Godfrey made no reply. And as he never came for his lesson, the professor became professor "emeritus."

The 13th of September was noted for one of the greatest and cruellest deceptions to which, on a desert island, the unfortunate survivors of a shipwreck could be subjected.

Godfrey had never again seen that inexplicable and undiscoverable smoke on the island; but on this day, about three o'clock in the afternoon, his attention was attracted by a long line of vapour, about the origin of which he could not be deceived.

He had gone for a walk to the end of Flag Point—the name which he had given to the cape on which he had erected his flagstaff. While he was looking through his glass he saw above the horizon a smoke driven by the west wind towards the island.

Godfrey's heart beat high.

"A ship!" he exclaimed.

But would this ship, this steamer, pass in sight of Phina Island? And if it passed, would it come near enough for the signal thereon to be seen on board?

Or would not rather the semi-visible smoke disappear with the vessel towards the north-west or south-west of the horizon?

For two hours Godfrey was a prey to alternating emotions more easy to indicate than to describe.

The smoke got bigger and bigger. It increased when the steamer re-stoked her fires, and diminished almost to vanishing-point as the fuel was consumed. Continually did the vessel visibly approach. About four o'clock her hull had come up on the line between the sky and the sea.

She was a large steamer, bearing north-east. Godfrey easily made that out. If that direction was maintained, she would inevitably approach Phina Island.

Godfrey had at first thought of running back to Will Tree to inform Tartlet. What was the use of doing so? The sight of one man making signals could do as much good as that of two. He remained there, his glass at his eye, losing not a single movement of the ship.

The steamer kept on her course towards the coast, her bow steered straight for the cape. By five o'clock the horizon-line was already above her hull, and her rig was visible. Godfrey could even recognize the colours at her gaff.

She carried the United States' ensign.

"But if I can see their flag, cannot they see mine? The wind keeps it out, so that they could easily see my flag with their glasses. Shall I make signals, by raising it and lowering it a few times, so as to show that I want to enter into communication with them? Yes! I have not an instant to lose."

It was a good idea. Godfrey ran to the end of Flag Point, and began to haul his flag up and down, as if he were saluting. Then he left it half-mast high, so as to show, in the way usual with seafaring people, that he required help and succour.

The steamer still approached to within three miles of the shore, but her flag remained immovable at the peak, and replied not to that on Flag Point. Godfrey felt his heart sink. He would not be noticed! It was half-past six, and the sun was about to set!

The steamer was now about two miles from the cape, which she was rapidly nearing. At this moment the sun disappeared below the horizon. With the first shadows of night, all hope of being seen had to be given up.

Godfrey again, with no more success, began to raise and lower his flag. There was no reply.

He then fired his gun two or three times, but the distance was still great, and the wind did not set in that direction! No report would be heard on board!

The night gradually came on; soon the steamer's hull grew invisible. Doubtless in another hour she would have passed Phina Island.

Godfrey, not knowing what to do, thought of setting fire to a group of resinous trees which grew at the back of Flag Point. He lighted a heap of dry leaves with some gunpowder, and then set light to the group of pines, which flared up like an enormous torch.

But no fire on the ship answered to the one on the land, and Godfrey returned sadly to Will Tree, feeling perhaps more desolate than he had ever felt till then.

CHAPTER XVI

IN WHICH SOMETHING HAPPENS WHICH CANNOT FAIL TO SURPRISE THE READER

To Godfrey the blow was serious. Would this unexpected chance which had just escaped him ever offer again? Could he hope so? No! The indifference of the steamer as she passed in sight of the island, without even taking a look at it, was obviously shared in by all the vessels venturing in this deserted portion of the Pacific. Why should they put into port more than she had done? The island did not possess a single harbour.

Godfrey passed a sorrowful night. Every now and then jumping up as if he heard a cannon out at sea, he would ask himself if the steamer had not caught sight of the huge fire which still burnt on the coast, and if she were not endeavouring to answer the signal by a gun-shot?

Godfrey listened. It was only an illusion of his over-excited brain. When the day came, he had come to look upon the apparition of the ship as but a dream, which had commenced about three o'clock on the previous afternoon.

But no! He was only too certain that a ship had been in sight of Phina Island, maybe within two miles of it, and certainly she had not put in.

Of this deception Godfrey said not a word to Tartlet. What was the good of talking about it? Besides, his frivolous mind could not see more than twenty-four hours ahead. He was no longer thinking of the chances of escaping from the island which might offer. He no longer imagined that the future had great things in store for them. San Francisco was fading out of his recollection. He had no sweetheart waiting for him, no Uncle Will to return to. If at this end of the world he could only commence a course of lessons on dancing, his happiness would be complete—were it only with one pupil.

If the professor dreamt not of immediate danger, such as to compromise his safety in this island—bare, as it was, of wild beasts and savages—he was wrong. This very day his optimism was to be put to a rude test.

About four o'clock in the afternoon Tartlet had gone, according to his custom, to collect some oysters and mussels, on that part of the shore behind Flag Point, when Godfrey saw him coming back as fast as his legs could carry him to Will Tree. His hair stood on end round his temples. He looked like a man in flight, who dared not turn his head to the right or to the left.

"What is the matter?" shouted Godfrey, not without alarm, running to meet his companion.

"There! there!" answered Tartlet, pointing with his finger towards the narrow strip of sea visible to the north between the trees.

"But what is it?" asked Godfrey, whose first movement was to run to the edge of the sequoias.

"A canoe!"

"A canoe?"

"Yes! Savages! Quite a fleet of savages! Cannibals, perhaps!"

Godfrey looked in the direction pointed out.

It was not a fleet, as the distracted Tartlet had said; but he was only mistaken about the quantity.

In fact, there was a small vessel gliding through the water, now very calm, about half-a-mile from the coast, so as to double Flag Point.

"And why should they be cannibals?" asked Godfrey, turning towards the professor.

"Because in Crusoe Islands," answered Tartlet, "there are always cannibals, who arrive sooner or later."

"Is it not a boat from some merchant-ship?"

"From a ship?"

"Yes. From a steamer which passed here yesterday afternoon, in sight of our island?"

"And you said nothing to me about it!" exclaimed Tartlet, lifting his hands to the sky.

"What good should I have done?" asked Godfrey. "Besides, I thought that the vessel had disappeared! But that boat might belong to her! Let us go and see!"

Godfrey ran rapidly back to Will Tree, and, seizing his glass, returned to the edge of the trees.

He then examined with extreme attention the little vessel, which would ere then have perceived the flag on Flag Point as it fluttered in the breeze.

The glass fell from his hands.

"Savages! Yes! They are really savages!" he exclaimed.

Tartlet felt his knees knock together, and a tremor of fright ran through his body.

It was a vessel manned by savages which Godfrey saw approaching the island. Built like a Polynesian canoe, she carried a large sail of woven bamboo; an outrigger on the weather side kept her from capsizing as she heeled down to the wind.

Godfrey easily distinguished the build of the vessel. She was a proa, and this would indicate that Phina Island was not far from Malaysia. But they were not Malays on board; they were half-naked blacks, and there were about a dozen of them.

The danger of being found was thus great. Godfrey regretted that he had hoisted the flag, which had not been seen by the ship, but would be by these black fellows. To take it down now would be too late.

It was, in truth, very unfortunate. The savages had probably come to the island thinking it was uninhabited, as indeed it had been before the wreck of the *Dream*. But there was the flag, indicating the presence of human beings on the coast! How were they to escape them if they landed?

Godfrey knew not what to do. Anyhow his immediate care must be to watch if they set foot on the island. He could think of other things afterwards.

With his glass at his eye he followed the proa; he saw it turn the point of the promontory, then run along the shore and then approach the mouth of the small stream, which, two miles up, flowed past Will Tree.

If the savages intended to paddle up the river, they would soon reach the group of sequoias—and nothing could hinder them. Godfrey and Tartlet ran rapidly back to their dwelling. They first of all set about guarding them selves against surprise, and giving themselves time to prepare their defence.

At least that is what Godfrey thought of. The ideas of the professor took quite a different turn.

"Ah!" he exclaimed. "It is destiny! This is as it was written? We could not escape it! You cannot be a Crusoe without a canoe coming to your island, without cannibals appearing one day or another! Here we have been for only three months, and there they are already! Assuredly, neither Defoe, nor De Wyss exaggerated matters! You can make yourself a Crusoe, if you like!"

Worthy Tartlet, folks do not make themselves Crusoes, they become Crusoes, and you are not sure that you are wise in comparing your position with that of the heroes of the two English and Swiss romances!

The precautions taken by Godfrey as soon as he returned to Will Tree were as follows. The fire burning among the roots of the sequoia was extinguished, and the embers scattered broadcast, so as to leave no trace; cocks, hens, and chickens were already in their house for the night, and the entrance was hidden with shrubs and twigs as much as possible; the other animals, the goats, agoutis, and sheep, were driven on to the prairie, but it was unlucky that there was no stable to shut them up in; all the instruments and tools were taken into the tree. Nothing was left outside that could indicate the presence or the passage of human beings.

Then the door was closely shut, after Godfrey and Tartlet had gone in. The door made of the sequoia bark was indistinguishable from the bark of the trunk, and might perhaps escape the eyes of the savages, who would not look at it very closely. It was the same with the two windows, in which the lower boards were shut. Then all light was extinguished in the dwelling, and our friends remained in total darkness. How long that night was! Godfrey and Tartlet heard the slightest sounds outside. The creaking of a dry branch, even a puff of wind, made them start. They thought they heard some one walking under the trees. It seemed that they were prowling round Will Tree. Then Godfrey climbed up to one of the windows, opened one of the boards, and anxiously peered into the gloom.

Nothing!

However, Godfrey at last heard footsteps on the ground. His ear could not deceive him this time. He still looked, but could only see one of the goats come for shelter beneath the trees.

Had any of the savages happened to discover the house hidden in the enormous sequoia, Godfrey had made up his mind what to do: he would drag up Tartlet with him by the chimney inside, and take refuge in the higher branches, where he would be better able to resist. With guns and revolvers in his possession, and ammunition in abundance, he would there have some chance against a dozen savages devoid of fire-arms.

If in the event of their being armed with bows and arrows they attacked from below, it was not likely that they would have the best of it against fire-arms aimed from above. If on the other hand they forced the door of the dwelling and tried to reach the branches from the inside, they would find it very difficult to get there, owing to the narrow opening, which the besieged could easily defend.

Godfrey said nothing about this to Tartlet. The poor man had been almost out of his mind with fright since he had seen the proa. The thought that he might be obliged to take refuge in the upper part of a tree, as if in an eagle's nest, would not have soothed him in the least. If it became necessary, Godfrey decided to drag him up before he had time to think about it.

The night passed amid these alternations of fear and hope. No attack occurred. The savages had not yet come to the sequoia group.

99

Perhaps they would wait for the day before venturing to cross the island.

"That is probably what they will do," said Godfrey, "since our flag shows that it is inhabited! But there are only a dozen of them, and they will have to be cautious! How are they to know that they have only to deal with a couple of shipwrecked men? No! They will risk nothing except by daylight—at least, if they are going to stop."

"Supposing they go away when the daylight comes?" answered Tartlet.

"Go away? Why should they have come to Phina Island for one night?"

"I do not know," replied the professor, who in his terror could only explain the arrival of the blacks by supposing that they had come to feed on human flesh.

"Anyhow," continued Godfrey; "to-morrow morning, if they have not come to Will Tree, we will go out and reconnoitre."

"We?"

"Yes! we! Nothing would be more imprudent than for us to separate! Who knows whether we may not have to run to the forest in the centre of the island and hide there for some days—until the departure of the proa! No! We will keep together, Tartlet!"

"Hush!" said the professor in a low voice; "I think I hear something outside."

Godfrey climbed up again to the window, and got down again almost immediately.

"No!" he said. "Nothing suspicious! It is only our cattle coming back to the wood."

"Hunted perhaps!" exclaimed Tartlet.

"They seem very quiet then," replied Godfrey; "I fancy they have only come in search of shelter against the morning dew."

"Ah!" murmured Tartlet in so piteous a tone that Godfrey could hardly help laughing, "these things could not happen at your uncle's place in Montgomery Street!"

"Day will soon break," said Godfrey, after a pause. "In an hour's time, if the savages have not appeared, we will leave Will Tree and reconnoitre towards the north of the island. You are able to carry a gun, Tartlet?"

"Carry? Yes!"

"And to fire it in a stated direction?"

"I do not know! I have never tried such a thing, and you may be sure, Godfrey, that my bullet will not go—"

"Who knows if the report alone might not frighten the savages?"

An hour later, it was light enough to see beyond the sequoias. Godfrey then cautiously reopened the shutters.

From that looking to the south he saw nothing extraordinary. The domestic animals wandered peacefully under the trees, and did not appear in the least alarmed. The survey completed, Godfrey carefully shut this window. Through the opening to the north there was a view up to the shore. Two miles off even the end of Flag Point could be seen; but the mouth of the river at the place where the savages had landed the evening before was not visible. Godfrey at first looked around without using his glass, so as to examine the environs of Will Tree on this side of Phina Island.

All was quite peaceful.

Godfrey then taking his glass swept round the coast to the promontory at Flag Point. Perhaps, as Tartlet had said, though it was difficult to find the reason, the savages had embarked, after a night spent on shore, without attempting to see if the island were inhabited.

CHAPTER XVII

IN WHICH PROFESSOR TARTLET'S GUN REALLY DOES MARVELS

But Godfrey suddenly uttered an exclamation which made the professor jump. There could be no doubt that the savages knew the island was inhabited, for the flag hitherto hoisted at the extremity of the cape had been carried away by them and no longer floated on the mast at Flag Point. The moment had then come to put the project into execution, to reconnoitre if the savages were still in the island, and to see what they were doing.

"Let us go," said he to his companion.

"Go! But—" answered Tartlet.

"Would you rather stay here?"

"With you, Godfrey—yes!"

"No—alone!"

"Alone! Never!"

"Come along then!"

Tartlet, thoroughly understanding that Godfrey would not alter his decision, resolved to accompany him. He had not courage enough to stay behind at Will Tree.

Before starting, Godfrey assured himself that the fire-arms were ready for action. The two guns were loaded, and one passed into the hands of the professor, who seemed as much embarrassed with it as might have been a savage of Pomotou. He also hung one of the hunting-knives to his belt, to which he had already attached his cartridge-pouch. The thought had occurred to him to also take his fiddle, imagining perhaps that they would be sensible to the charm of its squeaking, of which all the talent of a virtuoso could not conceal the harshness.

Godfrey had some trouble in getting him to abandon this idea, which was as ridiculous as it was impracticable.

It was now six o'clock in the morning. The summits of the sequoias were glowing in the first rays of the sun.

Godfrey opened the door; he stepped outside; he scanned the group of trees.

Complete solitude.

The animals had returned to the prairie. There they were, tranquilly browsing, about a quarter of a mile away. Nothing about them denoted the least uneasiness.

Godfrey made a sign to Tartlet to join him. The professor, as clumsy as could be in his fighting harness, followed—not without some hesitation.

Then Godfrey shut the door, and saw that it was well hidden in the bark of the sequoia. Then, having thrown at the foot of the tree a bundle of twigs, which he weighted with a few large stones, he set out towards the river, whose banks he intended to descend, if necessary, to its mouth. Tartlet followed him not without giving before each of his steps an uneasy stare completely round him up to the very limits of the horizon; but the fear of being left alone impelled him to advance.

Arrived at the edge of the group of trees, Godfrey stopped.

Taking his glasses from their case, he scanned with extreme attention all that part of the coast between the Flag Point promontory and the north-east angle of the island.

Not a living being showed itself, not a single smoke wreath was rising in the air.

The end of the cape was equally deserted, but they would there doubtless find numberless footprints freshly made. As for the mast, Godfrey had not been deceived. If the staff still rose above the last rock on the cape, it was bereft of its flag. Evidently the savages after coming to the place had gone off with the red cloth which had excited their covetousness, and had regained their boat at the mouth of the river.

Godfrey then turned off so as to examine the western shore.

It was nothing but a vast desert from Flag Point right away beyond the curve of Dream Bay.

No boat of any kind appeared on the surface of the sea. If the savages had taken to their proa, it only could be concluded that they were hugging the coast sheltered by the rocks, and so closely that they could not be seen.

However, Godfrey could not and would not remain in doubt. He was determined to ascertain, yes or no, if the proa had definitely left the island.

To do this it was necessary to visit the spot where the savages had landed the night before, that is to say, the narrow creek at the mouth of the river.

This he immediately attempted.

The borders of the small watercourse were shaded by occasional clumps of trees encircled by shrubs, for a distance of about two miles. Beyond that for some five or six hundred yards down to the sea the river ran between naked banks. This state of affairs enabled him to approach close to the landing-place without being perceived. It might be, however, that the savages had ascended the stream, and to be prepared for this eventuality the advance had to be made with extreme caution.

Godfrey, however thought, not without reason, that, at this early hour the savages, fatigued by their long voyage, would not have quitted their anchorage. Perhaps they were still sleeping either in their canoe or on land; in which case it would be seen if they could not be surprised.

This idea was acted upon at once. It was important that they should get on quickly. In such circumstances the advantage is generally gained at the outset. The fire-arms were again examined, the revolvers were carefully looked at, and then Godfrey and Tartlet commenced the descent of the left bank of the river in Indian file. All around was quiet. Flocks of birds flew from one bank to the other, pursuing each other among the higher branches without showing any uneasiness.

Godfrey went first, but it can easily be believed that his companion found the attempt to cover step rather tiring. Moving from one tree to another they advanced towards the shore without risk of discovery. Here the clumps of bushes hid them from the opposite bank, there even their heads disappeared amid the luxurious vegetation. But no matter where they were, an arrow from a bow or a stone from a sling might at any moment reach them. And so they had to be constantly on their guard.

However, in spite of the recommendations which were addressed to him, Tartlet, tripping against an occasional stump, had two or three falls which might have complicated matters. Godfrey was beginning to regret having brought such a clumsy assistant. Indeed, the poor man could not be much help to him. Doubtless he would have been worth more left behind at Will Tree; or, if he would not consent to that, hidden away in some nook in the forest. But it was too late. An hour after he had left the sequoia group, Godfrey and his companion had come a mile—only a mile—for the path was not easy beneath the high vegetation and between the luxuriant shrubs. Neither one nor the other of our friends had seen anything suspicious.

Hereabouts the trees thinned out for about a hundred yards or less, the river ran between naked banks, the country round was barer.

Godfrey stopped. He carefully observed the prairie to the right and left of the stream.

Still there was nothing to disquiet him, nothing to indicate the approach of savages. It is true that as they could not but believe the

104

island inhabited, they would not advance without precaution, in fact they would be as careful in ascending the little river as Godfrey was in descending it. It was to be supposed therefore that if they were prowling about the neighbourhood, they would also profit by the shelter of the trees or the high bushes of mastics and myrtles which formed such an excellent screen.

It was a curious though very natural circumstance that, the farther they advanced, Tartlet, perceiving no enemy, little by little lost his terror, and began to speak with scorn of "those cannibal laughing-stocks." Godfrey, on the contrary, became more anxious, and it was with greater precaution than ever that he crossed the open space and regained the shadow of the trees. Another hour led them to the place where the banks, beginning to feel the effects of the sea's vicinity, were only bordered with stunted shrubs, or sparse grasses.

Under these circumstances it was difficult to keep hidden or rather impossible to proceed without crawling along the ground.

This is what Godfrey did, and also what he advised Tartlet to do.

"There are not any savages! There are not any cannibals! They have all gone!" said the professor.

"There are!" answered Godfrey quickly, in a low voice, "They ought to be here! Down Tartlet, get down! Be ready to fire, but don't do so till I tell you."

Godfrey had said these words in such a tone of authority that the professor, feeling his limbs give way under him, had no difficulty in at once assuming the required position.

And he did well!

In fact, it was not without reason that Godfrey had spoken as he had.

From the spot which they then occupied, they could see neither the shore, nor the place where the river entered the sea. A small spur of hills shut out the view about a hundred yards ahead, but above this near horizon a dense smoke was rising straight in the air.

Godfrey, stretched at full length in the grass, with his finger on the trigger of his musket, kept looking towards the coast.

"This smoke," he said, "is it not of the same kind that I have already seen twice before? Should I conclude that savages have previously landed on the north and south of the island, and that the smoke came from fires lighted by them? But no! That is not possible, for I found no cinders, nor traces of a fireplace, nor embers! Ah! this time I'll know the reason of it."

And by a clever reptilian movement, which Tartlet imitated as well as he could, he managed, without showing his head above the grass, to reach the bend of the river.

Thence he could command, at his ease, every part of the bank through which the river ran.

An exclamation could not but escape him! His hand touched the professor's shoulder to prevent any movement of his! Useless to go further! Godfrey saw what he had come to see!

A large fire of wood was lighted on the beach, among the lower rocks, and from it a canopy of smoke rose slowly to the sky. Around the fire, feeding it with fresh armfuls of wood, of which they had made a heap, went and came the savages who had landed the evening before. Their canoe was moored to a large stone, and, lifted by the rising tide, oscillated on the ripples of the shore.

Godfrey could distinguish all that was passing on the sands without using his glasses. He was not more than two hundred yards from the fire, and he could even hear it crackling. He immediately perceived that he need fear no surprise from the rear, for all the blacks he had counted in the proa were in the group.

Ten out of the twelve were occupied in looking after the fire and sticking stakes in the ground with the evident intention of rigging up a spit in the Polynesian manner. An eleventh, who appeared to be the chief, was walking along the beach, and constantly turning his glances towards the interior of the island, as if he were afraid of an attack.

Godfrey recognized as a piece of finery on his shoulders the red stuff of his flag.

The twelfth savage was stretched on the ground, tied tightly to a post.

Godfrey recognized at once the fate in store for the wretched man. The spit was for him! The fire was to roast him at! Tartlet had not been mistaken, when, the previous evening, he had spoken of these folks as cannibals!

It must be admitted that neither was he mistaken in saying that the adventures of Crusoes, real or imaginary, were all copied one from the other!

Most certainly Godfrey and he did then find themselves in the same position as the hero of Daniel Defoe when the savages landed on his island. They were to assist, without doubt, at the same scene of cannibalism.

Godfrey decided to act as this hero did! He would not permit the massacre of the prisoner for which the stomachs of the cannibals were waiting! He was well armed. His two muskets—four shots—his two revolvers—a dozen shots—could easily settle these eleven rascals, whom the mere report of one of the fire-arms might perhaps be sufficient to scatter. Having taken his decision he coolly waited for the moment to interfere like a thunder-clap.

He had not long to wait!

Twenty minutes had barely elapsed, when the chief approached the fire. Then by a gesture he pointed out the prisoner to the savages who were expecting his orders.

Godfrey rose. Tartlet, without knowing why, followed the example. He did not even comprehend where his companion was going, for he had said nothing to him of his plans.

Godfrey imagined, evidently, that at sight of him the savages would make some movement, perhaps to rush to their boat, perhaps to rush at him.

They did nothing. It did not even seem as though they saw him; but at this moment the chief made a significant gesture. Three of his companions went towards the prisoner, unloosed him, and forced him near the fire.

He was still a young man, who, feeling that his last hour had come, resisted with all his might.

Assuredly, if he could, he would sell his life dearly. He began by throwing off the savages who held him, but he was soon knocked down, and the thief, seizing a sort of stone axe, jumped forward to beat in his head.

Godfrey uttered a cry, followed by a report. A bullet whistled through the air, and it seemed as though the chief were mortally wounded, for he fell on the ground.

At the report, the savages, surprised as though they had never heard the sound of fire-arms, stopped. At the sight of Godfrey those who held the prisoner instantly released him.

Immediately the poor fellow arose, and ran towards the place where he perceived his unexpected liberator.

At this moment a second report was heard.

It was Tartlet, who, without looking—for the excellent man kept his eyes shut—had just fired, and the stock of the musket on his right shoulder delivered the hardest knock which had ever been received by the professor of dancing and deportment.

But—what a chance it was!—a second savage fell close to his chief.

The rout at once began. Perhaps the savages thought they had to do with a numerous troop of natives whom they could not resist. Perhaps they were simply terrified at the sight of the two white men who seemed to keep the lightning in their pockets. There they were,

107

seizing the two who were wounded, carrying them off, rushing to the proa, driving it by their paddles out of the little creek, hoisting their sail, steering before the wind, making for the Flag Point promontory, and doubling it in hot haste.

Godfrey had no thought of pursuing them. What was the good of killing them? They had saved the victim. They had put them to flight, that was the important point. This had been done in such a way that the cannibals would never dare to return to Phina Island.

All was then for the best. They had only to rejoice in their victory, in which Tartlet did not hesitate to claim the greatest share.

Meanwhile the prisoner had come to his rescuer. For an instant he stopped, with the fear inspired in him by superior beings, but almost immediately he resumed his course. When he arrived before the two whites, he bowed to the ground; then catching hold of Godfrey's foot, he placed it on his head in sign of servitude.

One would almost have thought that this Polynesian savage had also read Robinson Crusoe!

CHAPTER XVIII

WHICH TREATS OF THE MORAL AND PHYSICAL EDUCATION OF A SIMPLE NATIVE OF THE PACIFIC

Godfrey at once raised the poor fellow, who lay prostrate before him. He looked in his face.

He was a man of thirty-five or more, wearing only a rag round his loins. In his features, as in the shape of his head, there could be recognized the type of the African negro. It was not possible to confound him with the debased wretches of the Polynesian islands, who, with their depressed crania and elongated arms, approach so strangely to the monkey.

Now, as he was a negro from Soudan or Abyssinia who had fallen into the hands of the natives of an archipelago of the Pacific, it might be that he could speak English or one or two words of the European languages which Godfrey understood. But it was soon apparent that the unhappy man only used an idiom that was absolutely incomprehensible—probably the language of the aborigines among whom he had doubtless arrived when very young. In fact, Godfrey had immediately interrogated him in English, and had obtained no reply. He then made him understand by signs, not without difficulty, that he would like to know his name.

After many fruitless essays, the negro, who had a very intelligent and even honest face, replied to the demand which was made of him in a single word,—

"Carefinotu."

"Carefinotu!" exclaimed Tartlet. "Do you hear the name? I propose that we call him 'Wednesday,' for to-day is Wednesday, and that is what they always do in these Crusoe islands! Is he to be allowed to call himself Carefinotu?"

"If that is his name," said Godfrey; "why should he not keep it?"

And at the moment he felt a hand placed on his chest, while all the black's physiognomy seemed to ask him what his name was.

"Godfrey!" answered he.

The black endeavoured to say the word, but although Godfrey repeated it several times, he could not succeed in pronouncing it in an intelligible fashion. Then he turned towards the professor, as if to know his name.

"Tartlet," was the reply of that individual in a most amiable tone.

"Tartlet!" repeated Carefinotu.

And it seemed as though this assemblage of syllables was more agreeable to his vocal chords, for he pronounced it distinctly.

The professor appeared to be extremely flattered. In truth he had reason to be.

Then Godfrey, wishing to put the intelligence of the black to some profit, tried to make him understand that he wished to know the name of the island. He pointed with his hand to the woods and prairies and hills, and then the shore which bound them, and then the horizon of the sea, and he interrogated him with a look.

Carefinotu did not at first understand what was meant, and imitating the gesture of Godfrey he also turned and ran his eyes over the space.

"Arneka," said he at length.

"Arneka?" replied Godfrey, striking the soil with his foot so as to accentuate his demand.

"Arneka!" repeated the negro.

This told Godfrey nothing, neither the geographical name borne by the island, nor its position in the Pacific. He could not remember such a name; it was probably a native one, little known to geographers.

However, Carefinotu did not cease from looking at the two white men, not without some stupor, going from one to the other as if he wished to fix in his mind the differences which characterized them. The smile on his mouth disclosed abundant teeth of magnificent whiteness which Tartlet did not examine without a certain reserve.

"If those teeth," he said, "have never eaten human flesh may my fiddle burst up in my hand."

"Anyhow, Tartlet," answered Godfrey; "our new companion no longer looks like the poor beggar they were going to cook and feed on! That is the main point!"

What particularly attracted the attention of Carefinotu were the weapons carried by Godfrey and Tartlet—as much the musket in the hand as the revolver in the belt.

Godfrey easily understood this sentiment of curiosity. It was evident that the savage had never seen a fire-arm. He said to himself that this was one of those iron tubes which had launched the thunder-bolt that had delivered him? There could be no doubt of it.

Godfrey, wishing to give him, not without reason, a high idea of the power of the whites, loaded his gun, and then, showing to

110

Carefinotu a red-legged partridge that was flying across the prairie about a hundred yards away, he shouldered it quickly, and fired. The bird fell.

At the report the black gave a prodigious leap, which Tartlet could not but admire from a choregraphic point of view. Then repressing his fear, and seeing the bird with broken wing running through the grass, he started off and swift as a greyhound ran towards it, and with many a caper, half of joy, half of stupefaction, brought it back to his master.

Tartlet then thought of displaying to Carefinotu that the Great Spirit had also favoured him with the power of the lightning; and perceiving a kingfisher tranquilly seated on an old stump near the river was bringing the stock up to his cheek, when Godfrey stopped him with,—

"No! Don't fire, Tartlet!"

"Why not?"

"Suppose that by some mishap you were not to hit the bird, think how we would fall in the estimation of the nigger!"

"And why should I not hit him?" replied Tartlet with some acerbity. "Did I not, during the battle, at more than a hundred paces, the very first time I handled a gun, hit one of the cannibals full in the chest?"

"You touched him evidently," said Godfrey; "for he fell. But take my advice, Tartlet, and in the common interest do not tempt fortune twice!"

The professor, slightly annoyed, allowed himself to be convinced; he threw the gun on to his shoulder with a swagger, and both our heroes, followed by Carefinotu, returned to Will Tree.

There the new guest of Phina Island met with quite a surprise in the habitation so happily contrived in the lower part of the sequoia. First he had to be shown, by using them while he looked on, the use of the tools, instruments, and utensils. It was obvious that Carefinotu belonged to, or had lived amongst savages in the lowest rank of the human scale, for fire itself seemed to be unknown to him. He could not understand why the pot did not take fire when they put it on the blazing wood; he would have hurried away from it, to the great displeasure of Tartlet, who was watching the different phases of the cooking of the soup. At a mirror, which was held out to him, he betrayed consummate astonishment; he turned round, and turned it round to see if he himself were not behind it.

"The fellow is hardly a monkey!" exclaimed the professor with a disdainful grimace.

111

"No, Tartlet," answered Godfrey; "he is more than a monkey, for his looks behind the mirror show good reasoning power."

"Well, I will admit that he is not a monkey," said Tartlet, shaking his head as if only half convinced; "but we shall see if such a being can be of any good to us."

"I am sure he will be!" replied Godfrey.

In any case Carefinotu showed himself quite at home with the food placed before him. He first tore it apart, and then tasted it; and then I believe that the whole breakfast of which they partook the—agouti soup, the partridge killed by Godfrey, and the shoulder of mutton with camas and yamph roots—would hardly have sufficed to calm the hunger which devoured him.

"The poor fellow has got a good appetite!" said Godfrey.

"Yes," responded Tartlet; "and we shall have to keep a watch on his cannibal instinct."

"Well, Tartlet! We shall make him get over the taste of human flesh if he ever had it!"

"I would not swear that," replied the professor. "It appears that once they have acquired this taste—"

While they were talking, Carefinotu was listening with extreme attention. His eyes sparkled with intelligence. One could see that he understood what was being said in his presence. He then spoke with extreme volubility, but it was only a succession of onomatopœias devoid of sense, of harsh interjections with *a* and *ou* predominant, as in the majority of Polynesian idioms.

Whatever the negro was, he was a new companion; he might become a devoted servant, which the most unexpected chance had sent to the hosts of Will Tree.

He was powerful, adroit, active; no work came amiss to him. He showed a real aptitude to imitate what he saw being done. It was in this way that Godfrey proceeded with his education. The care of the domestic animals, the collection of the roots and fruits, the cutting up of the sheep or agouties, which were to serve for food for the day, the fabrication of a sort of cider they extracted from the wild manzanilla apples,—he acquitted himself well in all these tasks, after having seen them done.

Whatever Tartlet thought, Godfrey felt no distrust in the savage, and never seemed to regret having come across him. What disquieted him was the possible return of the cannibals who now knew the situation of Phina Island.

From the first, a bed had been reserved for Carefinotu in the room at Will Tree, but generally, unless it was raining, he preferred to sleep outside in some hole in the tree, as though he were on guard over the house.

During the fortnight which followed his arrival on the island, Carefinotu many times accompanied Godfrey on his shooting excursions. His surprise was always extreme when he saw the game fall hit at such a distance; but in his character of retriever, he showed a dash and daring which no obstacles, hedge or bush, or stream, could stop.

Gradually, Godfrey became greatly attached to this negro. There was only one part of his progress in which Carefinotu showed refractoriness; that was in learning the English language. Do what he might he could not be prevailed upon to pronounce the most ordinary words which Godfrey, and particularly Professor Tartlet tried to teach him.

So the time passed. But if the present was fairly supportable, thanks to a happy accident, if no immediate danger menaced them, Godfrey could not help asking himself, if they were ever to leave this island, by what means they were to rejoin their country! Not a day passed but he thought of Uncle Will and his betrothed. It was not without secret apprehension that he saw the bad season approaching, which would put between his friends and him a barrier still more impassable.

On the 27th of September a circumstance occurred deserving of note.

If it gave more work to Godfrey and his two companions, it at least assured them of an abundant reserve of food.

Godfrey and Carefinotu were busied in collecting the mollusks, at the extreme end of Dream Bay, when they perceived out at sea an innumerable quantity of small moving islets which the rising tide was bringing gently to shore. It was a sort of floating archipelago, on the surface of which there walked, or flew, a few of those sea-birds, with great expanse of wing, known as sea-hawks.

What then were these masses which floated landwards, rising and falling with the undulations of the waves?

Godfrey did not know what to think, when Carefinotu threw himself down on his stomach, and then drawing his head back into his shoulders, folded beneath him his arms and legs, and began to imitate the movements of an animal crawling slowly along the ground.

Godfrey looked at him without understanding these extraordinary gymnastics. Then suddenly—

"Turtles!" he exclaimed.

113

Carefinotu was right. There was quite a square mile of myriads of turtles, swimming on the surface of the water.

About a hundred fathoms from the shore the greater part of them dived and disappeared, and the sea-hawks, finding their footing gone, flew up into the air in large spirals. But luckily about a hundred of the amphibians came on to the beach.

Godfrey and the negro had quickly run down in front of these creatures, each of which measured at the least from three to four feet in diameter. Now the only way of preventing turtles from regaining the sea is to turn them on their backs; and it was in this rough work that Godfrey and Carefinotu employed themselves, not without great fatigue.

The following days were spent in collecting the booty. The flesh of the turtle, which is excellent either fresh or preserved, could perhaps be kept for a time in both forms. In preparation for the winter, Godfrey had the greater part salted in such a way as to serve for the needs of each day. But for some time the table was supplied with turtle soup, on which Tartlet was not the only one to regale himself.

Barring this incident, the monotony of existence was in no way ruffled. Every day the same hours were devoted to the same work. Would not the life become still more depressing when the winter season would oblige Godfrey and his companions to shut themselves up in Will Tree? Godfrey could not think of it without anxiety. But what could he do?

Meanwhile, he continued the exploration of the island, and all the time not occupied with more pressing tasks he spent in roaming about with his gun. Generally Carefinotu accompanied him, Tartlet remaining behind at the dwelling. Decidedly he was no hunter, although his first shot had been a master-stroke!

Now on one of these occasions an unexpected incident happened, of a nature to gravely compromise the future safety of the inmates of Will Tree.

Godfrey and the black had gone out hunting in the central forest, at the foot of the hill which formed the principal ridge of Phina Island. Since the morning they had seen nothing pass but two or three antelopes through the high underwood, but at too great a distance for them to fire with any chance of hitting them.

As Godfrey was not in search of game for dinner, and did not seek to destroy for destruction's sake, he resigned himself to return empty-handed. If he regretted doing so it was not so much for the meat of the antelope, as for the skin, of which he intended to make good use.

It was about three o'clock in the afternoon. He and his companion after lunch were no more fortunate than before. They were preparing to return to Will Tree for dinner, when, just as they cleared the edge of the wood, Carefinotu made a bound; then precipitating himself on Godfrey, he seized him by the shoulders, and dragged him along with such vigour that resistance was impossible.

After going about twenty yards they stopped. Godfrey took breath, and, turning towards Carefinotu, interrogated him with a look.

The black, exceedingly frightened, stretched out his hand towards an animal which was standing motionless about fifty yards off.

It was a grizzly bear, whose paws held the trunk of a tree, and who was swaying his big head up and down, as if he were going to rush at the two hunters.

Immediately, without pausing to think, Godfrey loaded his gun, and fired before Carefinotu could hinder him.

Was the enormous plantigrade hit by the bullet? Probably. Was he killed? They could not be sure, but his paws unclasped, and he rolled at the foot of the tree. Delay was dangerous. A struggle with so formidable an animal might have the worst results. In the forests of California the pursuit of the grizzly is fraught with the greatest danger, even to professional hunters of the beast.

And so the black seized Godfrey by the arms to drag him away in the direction of Will Tree, and Godfrey, understanding that he could not be too cautious, made no resistance.

CHAPTER XIX

IN WHICH THE SITUATION ALREADY GRAVELY COMPROMISED BECOMES MORE AND MORE COMPLICATED

The presence of a formidable wild beast in Phina Island was, it must be confessed, calculated to make our friends think the worst of the ill-fortune which had fallen on them.

Godfrey—perhaps he was wrong—did not consider that he ought to hide from Tartlet what had passed.

"A bear!" screamed the professor, looking round him with a bewildered glare as if the environs of Will Tree were being assailed by a herd of wild beasts. "Why, a bear? Up to now we had not even got a bear in our island! If there is one there may be many, and even numbers of other ferocious beasts—jaguars, panthers, tigers, hyænas, lions!"

Tartlet already beheld Phina Island given over to quite a menagerie escaped from their cages.

Godfrey answered that there was no need for him to exaggerate. He had seen one bear, that was certain. Why one of these animals had never been seen before in his wanderings on the island he could not explain, and it was indeed inexplicable. But to conclude from this that wild animals of all kinds were prowling in the woods and prairies was to go too far. Nevertheless, they would have to be cautious and never go out unarmed.

Unhappy Tartlet! From this day there commenced for him an existence of anxieties, emotions, alarms, and irrational terrors which gave him nostalgia for his native land in a most acute form.

"No!" repeated he. "No! If there are animals—I have had enough of it, and I want to get off!"

He had not the power.

Godfrey and his companions then had henceforth to be on their guard. An attack might take place not only on the shore side or the prairie side, but even in the group of sequoias. This is why serious measures were taken to put the habitation in a state to repel a sudden attack. The door was strengthened, so as to resist the clutches of a wild beast. As for the domestic animals Godfrey would have built a stable to shut them up in at least at night, but it was not easy to do so. He contented himself at present with making a sort of enclosure of branches not far from Will Tree, which would keep them as in a fold. But the enclosure was not solid enough nor high enough to hinder a bear or hyæna from upsetting it or getting over it.

Notwithstanding the remonstrances made to him, Carefinotu persisted in watching outside during the night, and Godfrey hoped thus to receive warning of a direct attack.

Decidedly Carefinotu endangered his life in thus constituting himself the guardian of Will Tree; but he had understood that he could thus be of service to his liberators, and he persisted, in spite of all Godfrey said to him, in watching as usual over the general safety.

A week passed without any of these formidable visitors appearing in the neighbourhood. Godfrey did not go very far from the dwelling, unless there was a necessity for his doing so. While the sheep and goats grazed on the neighbouring prairie, they were never allowed out of sight. Generally Carefinotu acted as shepherd. He did not take a gun, for he did not seem to understand the management of fire-arms, but one of the hunting-knives hung from his belt, and he carried an axe in his right hand. Thus armed the active negro would not have hesitated to throw himself before a tiger or any animal of the worst description.

However, as neither a bear nor any of his congeners had appeared since the last encounter Godfrey began to gather confidence. He gradually resumed his hunting expeditions, but without pushing far into the interior of the island. Frequently the black accompanied him; Tartlet, safe in Will Tree, would not risk himself in the open, not even if he had the chance of giving a dancing lesson. Sometimes Godfrey would go alone, and then the professor had a companion to whose instruction he obstinately devoted himself.

Yes! Tartlet had at first thought of teaching Carefinotu the most ordinary words in the English language, but he had to give this up, as the negro seemed to lack the necessary phonetic apparatus for that kind of pronunciation. "Then," had Tartlet said, "if I cannot be his professor, I will be his pupil!"

And he it was who attempted to learn the idiom spoken by Carefinotu. Godfrey had warned him that the accomplishment would be of little use. Tartlet was not dissuaded. He tried to get Carefinotu to name the objects he pointed at with his hand. In truth Tartlet must have got on excellently, for at the end of fifteen days he actually knew fifteen words! He knew that Carefinotu said "birsi" for fire, "aradore" for the sky, "mervira" for the sea, "doura" for a tree, &c. He was as proud of this as if he had taken the first prize for Polynesian at some examination!

117

It was then with a feeling of gratitude that he wished to make some recognition of what had been done for him, and instead of torturing the negro with English words, he resolved on teaching him deportment and the true principles of European choregraphy.

At this Godfrey could not restrain his peals of laughter. After all it would pass the time away, and on Sunday, when there was nothing else to do, he willingly assisted at the course of lectures delivered by the celebrated Professor Tartlet of San Francisco. Indeed, we ought to have seen them! The unhappy Carefinotu perspired profusely as he went through the elementary exercises. He was docile and willing, nevertheless; but like all his fellows, his shoulders did not set back, nor did his chest throw out, nor did his knees or his feet point apart! To make a Vestris or a Saint Leon of a savage of this sort!

The professor pursued his task in quite a fury. Carefinotu, tortured as he was, showed no lack of zeal. What he suffered, even to get his feet into the first position can be imagined! And when he passed to the second and then to the third, it was still more agonizing.

"But look at me, you blockhead!" exclaimed Tartlet, who added example to precept. "Put your feet out! Further out! The heel of one to the heel of the other! Open your knees, you duffer! Put back your shoulders, you idiot! Stick up your head! Round your elbows!"

"But you ask what is impossible!" said Godfrey.

"Nothing is impossible to an intelligent man!" was Tartlet's invariable response.

"But his build won't allow of it."

"Well, his build must allow of it! He will have to do it sooner or later, for the savage must at least know how to present himself properly in a drawing-room!"

"But, Tartlet, he will never have the opportunity of appearing in a drawing-room!"

"Eh! How do you know that, Godfrey?" replied the professor, drawing himself up. "Do you know what the future may bring forth?"

This was the last word in all discussions with Tartlet. And then the professor taking his kit would with the bow extract from it some squeaky little air to the delight of Carefinotu. It required but this to excite him. Oblivious of choregraphic rules, what leaps, what contortions, what capers!

And Tartlet, in a reverie, as he saw this child of Polynesia so demean himself, inquired if these steps, perhaps a little too characteristic, were not natural to the human being, although outside all the principles of his art.

But we must leave the professor of dancing and deportment to his philosophical meditations, and return to questions at once more practical and pressing.

During his last excursions into the plain, either by himself or with Carefinotu, Godfrey had seen no wild animal. He had even come upon no traces of such. The river to which they would come to drink bore no footprint on its banks. During the night there were no howlings nor suspicious noises. Besides the domestic animals continued to give no signs of uneasiness.

"This is singular," said Godfrey several times; "but I was not mistaken! Carefinotu certainly was not! It was really a bear that he showed me! It was really a bear that I shot! Supposing I killed him, was he the last representative of the plantigrades on the island?"

It was quite inexplicable! Besides, if Godfrey had killed this bear, he would have found the body where he had shot it. Now they searched for it in vain! Were they to believe then that the animal mortally wounded had died far off in some den. It was possible after all, but then at this place, at the foot of this tree, there would have been traces of blood, and there were none.

"Whatever it is," thought Godfrey, "it does not much matter; and we must keep on our guard."

With the first days of November it could be said that the wet season had commenced in this unknown latitude. Cold rains fell for many hours. Later on probably they would experience those interminable showers which do not cease for weeks at a time, and are characteristic of the rainy period of winter in these latitudes.

Godfrey had then to contrive a fireplace in the interior of Will Tree—an indispensable fireplace that would serve as well to warm the dwelling during the winter months as to cook their food in shelter from the rain and tempest.

The hearth could at any time be placed in a corner of the chamber between big stones, some placed on the ground and others built up round them; but the question was how to get the smoke out, for to leave it to escape by the long chimney, which ran down the centre of the sequoia, proved impracticable.

Godfrey thought of using as a pipe some of those long stout bamboos which grew on certain parts of the river banks. It should be said that on this occasion he was greatly assisted by Carefinotu. The negro, not without effort, understood what Godfrey required. He it was who accompanied him for a couple of miles from Will Tree to select the larger bamboos, he it was who helped him build his hearth. The stones were placed on the ground opposite to the door; the bamboos, emptied of their pith and bored through at the knots, afforded, when joined one to another, a tube of sufficient length, which ran out through an aperture made for it in the sequoia bark, and would serve every purpose, provided it did not catch fire. Godfrey soon had the satisfaction of seeing a good fire burning without filling the interior of Will Tree with smoke.

He was quite right in hastening on these preparations, for from the 3rd to the 10th of November the rain never ceased pouring down. It would have been impossible to keep a fire going in the open air. During these miserable days they had to keep indoors and did got venture out except when the flocks and poultry urgently required them to do so. Under these circumstances the reserve of camas roots began to fail; and these were what took the place of bread, and of which the want would be immediately felt.

Godfrey then one day, the 10th of November, informed Tartlet that as soon as the weather began to mend a little he and Carefinotu would go out and collect some. Tartlet, who was never in a hurry to run a couple of miles across a soaking prairie, decided to remain at home during Godfrey's absence.

In the evening the sky began to clear of the heavy clouds which the west wind had been accumulating since the commencement of the month, the rain gradually ceased, the sun gave forth a few crepuscular rays. It was to be hoped that the morning would yield a lull in the storm, of which it was advisable to make the most.

"To-morrow," said Godfrey, "I will go out, and Carefinotu will go with me."

"Agreed!" answered Tartlet.

The evening came, and when supper was finished and the sky, cleared of clouds, permitted a few brilliant stars to appear, the black wished to take up his accustomed place outside, which he had had to abandon during the preceding rainy nights. Godfrey tried to make him understand that he had better remain indoors, that there was no necessity to keep a watch as no wild animal had been noticed; but Carefinotu was obstinate. He therefore had to have his way.

The morning was as Godfrey had foreseen, no rain had fallen since the previous evening, and when he stepped forth from Will Tree, the first rays of the sun were lightly gilding the thick dome of the sequoias.

Carefinotu was at his post, where he had passed the night. He was waiting. Immediately, well armed and provided with large

120

sacks, the two bid farewell to Tartlet, and started for the river, which they intended ascending along the left bank up to the camas bushes.

An hour afterwards they arrived there without meeting with any unpleasant adventure.

The roots were rapidly torn up and a large quantity obtained, so as to fill the sacks. This took three hours, so that it was about eleven o'clock in the morning when Godfrey and his companion set out on their return to Will Tree.

Walking close together, keeping a sharp look-out, for they could not talk to each other, they had reached a bend in the small river where there were a few large trees, grown like a natural cradle across the stream, when Godfrey suddenly stopped.

This time it was he who showed to Carefinotu a motionless animal at the foot of a tree whose eyes were gleaming with a singular light.

"A tiger!" he exclaimed.

He was not mistaken. It was really a tiger of large stature resting on its hind legs with its forepaws on the trunk of a tree, and ready to spring.

In a moment Godfrey had dropped his sack of roots. The loaded gun passed into his right hand; he cocked it, presented it, aimed it, and fired.

"Hurrah! hurrah!" he exclaimed.

This time there was no room for doubt; the tiger, struck by the bullet, had bounded backwards. But perhaps he was not mortally wounded, perhaps rendered still more furious by his wound he would spring on to them!

Godfrey held his gun pointed, and threatened the animal with his second barrel.

But before Godfrey could stop him, Carefinotu had rushed at the place where the tiger disappeared, his hunting-knife in his hand.

Godfrey shouted for him to stop, to come back! It was in vain. The black, resolved even at the risk of his life to finish the animal which perhaps was only wounded, did not or would not hear.

Godfrey rushed after him.

When he reached the bank, he saw Carefinotu struggling with the tiger, holding him by the throat, and at last stabbing him to the heart with a powerful blow.

The tiger then rolled into the river, of which the waters, swollen by the rains, carried it away with the quickness of a torrent. The corpse, which floated only for an instant, was swiftly borne off towards the sea.

A bear! A tiger! There could be no doubt that the island did contain formidable beasts of prey!

Godfrey, after rejoining Carefinotu, found that in the struggle the black had only received a few scratches. Then, deeply anxious about the future, he retook the road to Will Tree.

CHAPTER XX

IN WHICH TARTLET REITERATES IN EVERY KEY THAT HE WOULD RATHER BE OFF

When Tartlet learnt that there were not only bears in the island, but tigers too, his lamentations again arose. Now he would never dare to go out! The wild beasts would end by discovering the road to Will Tree! There was no longer any safety anywhere! In his alarm the professor wanted for his protection quite a fortification! Yes! Stone walls with scarps and counterscarps, curtains and bastions, and ramparts, for what was the use of a shelter under a group of sequoias? Above all things, he would at all risks, like to be off.

"So would I," answered Godfrey quietly.

In fact, the conditions under which the castaways on Phina Island had lived up to now were no longer the same. To struggle to the end, to struggle for the necessaries of life, they had been able, thanks to fortunate circumstances. Against the bad season, against winter and its menaces, they knew how to act, but to have to defend themselves against wild animals, whose attack was possible every minute, was another thing altogether; and in fact they could not do it.

The situation, already complicated, had become very serious, for it had become intolerable.

"But," repeated Godfrey to himself, without cessation, "how is it that for four months we did not see a single beast of prey in the island, and why during the last fortnight have we had to encounter a bear and a tiger? What shall we say to that?"

The fact might be inexplicable, but it was none the less real.

Godfrey, whose coolness and courage increased, as difficulties grew, was not cast down. If dangerous animals menaced their little colony, it was better to put themselves on guard against their attacks, and that without delay.

But what was to be done?

It was at the outset decided that excursions into the woods or to the sea-shore should be rarer, and that they should never go out unless well armed, and only when it was absolutely necessary for their wants.

"We have been lucky enough in our two encounters!" said Godfrey frequently; "but there may come a time when we may not

123

shoot so straight! So there is no necessity for us to run into danger!"

At the same time they had not only to settle about the excursions, but to protect Will Tree—not only the dwelling, but the annexes, the poultry roost, and the fold for the animals, where the wild beasts could easily cause irreparable disaster.

Godfrey thought then, if not of fortifying Will Tree according to the famous plans of Tartlet, at least of connecting the four or five large sequoias which surrounded it.

If he could devise a high and strong palisade from one tree to another, they would be in comparative security at any rate from a surprise.

It was practicable—Godfrey concluded so after an examination of the ground—but it would cost a good deal of labour. To reduce this as much as possible, he thought of erecting the palisade around a perimeter of only some three hundred feet. We can judge from this the number of trees he had to select, cut down, carry, and trim until the enclosure was complete.

Godfrey did not quail before his task. He imparted his projects to Tartlet, who approved them, and promised his active co-operation; but what was more important, he made his plans understood to Carefinotu, who was always ready to come to his assistance.

They set to work without delay.

There was at a bend in the stream, about a mile from Will Tree, a small wood of stone pines of medium height, whose trunks, in default of beams and planks, without wanting to be squared, would, by being placed close together, form a solid palisade.

It was to this wood that, at dawn on the 12th of November, Godfrey and his two companions repaired. Though well armed they advanced with great care.

"You can have too much of this sort of thing," murmured Tartlet, whom these new difficulties had rendered still more discontented, "I would rather be off!"

But Godfrey did not take the trouble to reply to him.

On this occasion his tastes were not being consulted, his intelligence even was not being appealed to. It was the assistance of his arms that the common interest demanded. In short, he had to resign himself to his vocation of beast of burden.

No unpleasant accident happened in the mile which separated the wood from Will Tree. In vain they had carefully beaten the underwood, and swept the horizon all around them. The domestic animals they had left out at pasture gave no sign of alarm. The birds continued their frolics with no more anxiety than usual.

Work immediately began. Godfrey, very properly did not want to begin carrying until all the trees he wanted had been felled. They could work at them in greater safety on the spot.

Carefinotu was of great service during this toilsome task. He had become very clever in the use of the axe and saw. His strength even allowed him to continue at work when Godfrey was obliged to rest for a minute or so, and when Tartlet, with bruised hands and aching limbs, had not even strength left to lift his fiddle.

However, although the unfortunate professor of dancing and deportment had been transformed into a wood-cutter, Godfrey had reserved for him the least fatiguing part, that is, the clearing off of the smaller branches. In spite of this, if Tartlet had only been paid half a dollar a day, he would have stolen four-fifths of his salary!

For six days, from the 12th to the 17th of November, these labours continued. Our friends went off in the morning at dawn, they took their food with them, and they did not return to Will Tree until evening. The sky was not very clear. Heavy clouds frequently accumulated over it. It was harvest weather, with alternating showers and sunshine; and during the showers the wood-cutters would take shelter under the trees, and resume their task when the rain had ceased.

On the 18th all the trees, topped and cleared of branches, were lying on the ground, ready for transport to Will Tree.

During this time no wild beast had appeared in the neighbourhood of the river. The question was, were there any more in the island, or had the bear and the tiger been—a most improbable event—the last of their species?

Whatever it was, Godfrey had no intention of abandoning his project of the solid palisade so as to be prepared against a surprise from savages, or bears, or tigers. Besides, the worst was over, and there only remained to take the wood where it was wanted.

We say "the worst was over," though the carriage promised to be somewhat laborious. If it were not so, it was because Godfrey had had a very practical idea, which materially lightened the task; this was to make use of the current of the river, which the flood occasioned by the recent rains had rendered very rapid, to transport the wood. Small rafts could be formed, and they would quietly float down to the sequoias, where a bar, formed by the small bridge, would stop them. From thence to Will Tree was only about fifty-five paces.

If any of them showed particular satisfaction at this mode of procedure, it was Tartlet.

On the 18th the first rafts were formed, and they arrived at the barrier without accident. In less than three days on the evening of the 25th, the palisade had been all sent down to its destination.

On the morrow, the first trunks, sunk two feet in the soil, began to rise in such a manner as to connect the principal sequoias which surrounded Will Tree. A capping of strong flexible branches, pointed by the axe, assured the solidity of the wall.

Godfrey saw the work progress with extreme satisfaction, and delayed not until it was finished.

"Once the palisade is done," he said to Tartlet, "we shall be really at home."

"We shall not be really at home," replied the professor drily, "until we are in Montgomery Street, with your Uncle Kolderup."

There was no disputing this opinion.

On the 26th of November the palisade was three parts done. It comprised among the sequoias attached one to another that in which the poultry had established themselves, and Godfrey's intention was to build a stable inside it.

In three or four days the fence was finished. There only remained to fit in a solid door, which would assure the closure of Will Tree.

But on the morning of the 27th of November the work was interrupted by an event which we had better explain with some detail, for it was one of those unaccountable things peculiar to Phina Island.

About eight o'clock, Carefinotu had climbed up to the fork of the sequoia, so as to more carefully close the hole by which the cold and rain penetrated, when he uttered a singular cry.

Godfrey, who was at work at the palisade, raised his head and saw the black, with expressive gestures, motioning to him to join him without delay.

Godfrey, thinking Carefinotu would not have disturbed him unless he had serious reason, took his glasses with him and climbed up the interior passage, and passing through the hole, seated himself astride of one of the main branches.

Carefinotu, pointing with his arm towards the rounded angle which Phina Island made to the north-east, showed a column of smoke rising in the air like a long plume.

"Again!" exclaimed Godfrey.

And putting his glasses in the direction, he assured himself that this time there was no possible error, that it must escape from

126

some important fire, which he could distinctly see must be about five miles off.

Godfrey turned towards the black.

Carefinotu expressed his surprise, by his looks, his exclamations, in fact by his whole attitude.

Assuredly he was no less astounded than Godfrey at this apparition.

Besides, in the offing, there was no ship, not a vessel native or other, nothing which showed that a landing had recently been made on the shore.

"Ah! This time I will find out the fire which produces that smoke!" exclaimed Godfrey.

And pointing to the north-east angle of the island, and then to the foot of the tree, he gesticulated to Carefinotu that he wished to reach the place without losing an instant.

Carefinotu understood him. He even gave him to understand that he approved of the idea.

"Yes," said Godfrey to himself, "if there is a human being there, we must know who he is and whence he comes! We must know why he hides himself! It will be for the safety of all!"

A moment afterwards Carefinotu and he descended to the foot of Will Tree. Then Godfrey, informing Tartlet of what had passed and what he was going to do, proposed for him to accompany them to the north coast.

A dozen miles to traverse in one day was not a very tempting suggestion to a man who regarded his legs as the most precious part of his body, and only designed for noble exercises. And so he replied that he would prefer to remain at Will Tree.

"Very well, we will go alone," answered Godfrey, "but do not expect us until the evening."

So saying, and Carefinotu and he carrying some provisions for lunch on the road, they set out, after taking leave of the professor, whose private opinion it was that they would find nothing, and that all their fatigue would be useless.

Godfrey took his musket and revolver; the black the axe and the hunting-knife which had become his favourite weapon. They crossed the plank bridge to the right bank of the river, and then struck off across the prairie to the point on the shore where the smoke had been seen rising amongst the rocks.

It was rather more easterly than the place which Godfrey had uselessly visited on his second exploration.

They progressed rapidly, not without a sharp look-out that the

127

wood was clear and that the bushes and underwood did not hide some animal whose attack might be formidable.

Nothing disquieting occurred.

At noon, after having had some food, without, however, stopping for an instant, they reached the first line of rocks which bordered the beach. The smoke, still visible, was rising about a quarter of a mile ahead. They had only to keep straight on to reach their goal.

They hastened their steps, but took precautions so as to surprise, and not be surprised.

Two minutes afterwards the smoke disappeared, as if the fire had been suddenly extinguished.

But Godfrey had noted with exactness the spot whence it arose. It was at the point of a strangely formed rock, a sort of truncated pyramid, easily recognizable. Showing this to his companion, he kept straight on.

The quarter of a mile was soon traversed, then the last line was climbed, and Godfrey and Carefinotu gained the beach about fifty paces from the rock.

They ran up to it. Nobody! But this time half-smouldering embers and half-burnt wood proved clearly that the fire had been alight on the spot.

"There has been some one here!" exclaimed Godfrey. "Some one not a moment ago! We must find out who!"

He shouted. No response! Carefinotu gave a terrible yell. No one appeared!

Behold them then hunting amongst the neighbouring rocks, searching a cavern, a grotto, which might serve as a refuge for a shipwrecked man, an aboriginal, a savage—

It was in vain that they ransacked the slightest recesses of the shore. There was neither ancient nor recent camp in existence, not even the traces of the passage of a man.

"But," repeated Godfrey, "it was not smoke from a warm spring this time! It was from a fire of wood and grass, and that fire could not light itself."

Vain was their search. Then about two o'clock Godfrey and Carefinotu, as weary as they were disconcerted at their fruitless endeavours, retook their road to Will Tree.

There was nothing astonishing in Godfrey being deep in thought. It seemed to him that the island was now under the empire of some occult power. The reappearance of this fire, the presence of wild animals, did not all this denote some extraordinary complication?

128

And was there not cause for his being confirmed in this idea when an hour after he had regained the prairie, he heard a singular noise, a sort of hard jingling.

Carefinotu pushed him aside at the same instant as a serpent glided beneath the herbage, and was about to strike at him.

"Snakes, now. Snakes in the island, after the bears and the tigers!" he exclaimed.

Yes! It was one of those reptiles well-known by the noise they make, a rattlesnake of the most venomous species: a giant of the Crotalus family!

Carefinotu threw himself between Godfrey and the reptile, which hurried off under a thick bush.

But the negro pursued it and smashed in its head with a blow of the axe. When Godfrey rejoined him, the two halves of the reptile were writhing on the blood-stained soil.

Then other serpents, not less dangerous, appeared in great abundance on this part of the prairie which was separated by the stream from Will Tree.

Was it then a sudden invasion of reptiles? Was Phina Island going to become the rival of ancient Tenos, whose formidable ophidians rendered it famous in antiquity, and which gave its name to the viper?

"Come on! come on!" exclaimed Godfrey, motioning to Carefinotu to quicken the pace.

He was uneasy. Strange presentiments agitated him without his being able to control them.

Under their influence, fearing some approaching misfortune, he had hastened his return to Will Tree.

But matters became serious when he reached the planks across the river.

Screams of terror resounded from beneath the sequoias—cries for help in a tone of agony which it was impossible to mistake!

"It is Tartlet!" exclaimed Godfrey. "The unfortunate man has been attacked! Quick! quick!"

Once over the bridge, about twenty paces further on, Tartlet was perceived running as fast as his legs could carry him.

An enormous crocodile had come out of the river and was pursuing him with its jaws wide open. The poor man, distracted, mad with fright, instead of turning to the right or the left, was keeping in a straight line, and so running the risk of being caught. Suddenly he stumbled. He fell. He was lost.

Godfrey halted. In the presence of this imminent danger his coolness never forsook him for an instant. He brought his gun to his

129

shoulder, and aimed at the crocodile. The well-aimed bullet struck the monster, and it made a bound to one side and fell motionless on the ground.

Carefinotu rushed towards Tartlet and lifted him up. Tartlet had escaped with a fright! But what a fright!

It was six o'clock in the evening.

A moment afterwards Godfrey and his two companions had reached Will Tree.

How bitter were their reflections during their evening repast! What long sleepless hours were in store for the inhabitants of Phina Island, on whom misfortunes were now crowding.

As for the professor, in his anguish he could only repeat the words which expressed the whole of his thoughts, "I had much rather be off!"

CHAPTER XXI

WHICH ENDS WITH QUITE A SURPRISING REFLECTION BY THE NEGRO CAREFINOTU

The winter season, so severe in these latitudes, had come at last. The first frosts had already been felt, and there was every promise of rigorous weather. Godfrey was to be congratulated on having established his fireplace in the tree. It need scarcely be said that the work at the palisade had been completed, and that a sufficiently solid door now assured the closure of the fence.

During the six weeks which followed, that is to say, until the middle of December, there had been a good many wretched days on which it was impossible to venture forth. At the outset there came terrible squalls. They shook the group of sequoias to their very roots. They strewed the ground with broken branches, and so furnished an ample reserve for the fire.

Then it was that the inhabitants of Will Tree clothed themselves as warmly as they could. The woollen stuffs found in the box were used during the few excursions necessary for revictualling, until the weather became so bad that even these were forbidden. All hunting was at an end, and the snow fell in such quantity that Godfrey could have believed himself in the inhospitable latitudes of the Arctic Ocean.

It is well known that Northern America, swept by the Polar winds, with no obstacle to check them, is one of the coldest countries on the globe. The winter there lasts until the month of April. Exceptional precautions have to be taken against it. It was the coming of the winter as it did which gave rise to the thought that Phina Island was situated in a higher latitude than Godfrey had supposed.

Hence the necessity of making the interior of Will Tree as comfortable as possible. But the suffering from rain and cold was cruel. The reserves of provisions were unfortunately insufficient, the preserved turtle flesh gradually disappeared. Frequently there had to be sacrificed some of the sheep or goats or agouties, whose numbers had but slightly increased since their arrival in the island.

With these new trials, what sad thoughts haunted Godfrey!

It happened also that for a fortnight he fell into a violent fever. Without the tiny medicine-chest which afforded the necessary drugs for his treatment, he might never have recovered. Tartlet was ill-suited to attend to the petty cares that were necessary during the continuance of the malady. It was to Carefinotu that he mainly owed his return to health.

But what remembrances and what regrets! Who but himself could he blame for having got into a situation of which he could not even see the end? How many times in his delirium did he call Phina, whom he never should see again, and his Uncle Will, from whom he beheld himself separated for ever! Ah! he had to alter his opinion of this Crusoe life which his boyish imagination had made his ideal! Now he was contending with reality! He could no longer even hope to return to the domestic hearth.

So passed this miserable December, at the end of which Godfrey began to recover his strength.

As for Tartlet, by special grace, doubtless, he was always well. But what incessant lamentations! What endless jeremiads! As the grotto of Calypso after the departure of Ulysses, Will Tree "resounded no more to his song"—that of his fiddle—for the cold had frozen the strings!

It should be said too that one of the gravest anxieties of Godfrey was not only the re-appearance of dangerous animals, but the fear of the savages returning in great numbers to Phina Island, the situation of which was known to them. Against such an invasion the palisade was but an insufficient barrier. All things considered, the refuge offered by the high branches of the sequoia appeared much safer, and the rendering the access less difficult was taken in hand. It would always be easy to defend the narrow orifice by which the top of the trunk was reached.

With the aid of Carefinotu Godfrey began to cut regular ledges on each side, like the steps of a staircase, and these, connected by a long cord of vegetable fibre, permitted of rapid ascent up the interior.

"Well," said Godfrey, when the work was done, "that gives us a town house below and a country house above!"

"I had rather have a cellar, if it was in Montgomery Street!" answered Tartlet.

Christmas arrived. Christmas kept in such style throughout the United States of America! The New Year's Day, full of memories of childhood, rainy, snowy, cold, and gloomy, began the new year under the most melancholy auspices.

It was six months since the survivors of the *Dream* had remained without communication with the rest of the world.

The commencement of the year was not very cheering. It

132

made Godfrey and his companions anticipate that they would still have many trials to encounter.

The snow never ceased falling until January 18th. The flocks had to be let out to pasture to get what feed they could. At the close of the day, a very cold damp night enveloped the island, and the space shaded by the sequoias was plunged in profound obscurity.

Tartlet and Carefinotu, stretched on their beds inside Will Tree, were trying in vain to sleep. Godfrey, by the struggling light of a torch, was turning over the pages of his Bible.

About ten o'clock a distant noise, which came nearer and nearer, was heard outside away towards the north. There could be no mistake. It was the wild beasts prowling in the neighbourhood, and, alarming to relate, the howling of the tiger and of the hyæna, and the roaring of the panther and the lion were this time blended in one formidable concert.

Godfrey, Tartlet, and the negro sat up, each a prey to indescribable anguish. If at this unaccountable invasion of ferocious animals Carefinotu shared the alarm of his companions, his astonishment was quite equal to his fright.

During two mortal hours all three kept on the alert. The howlings sounded at times close by; then they suddenly ceased, as if the beasts, not knowing the country, were roaming about all over it. Perhaps then Will Tree would escape an attack!

"It doesn't matter if it does," thought Godfrey. "If we do not destroy these animals to the very last one, there will be no safety for us in the island!"

A little after midnight the roaring began again in full strength at a moderate distance away. Impossible now to doubt but that the howling army was approaching Will Tree!

Yes! It was only too certain! But whence came these wild animals? They could not have recently landed on Phina Island! They must have been there then before Godfrey's arrival! But how was it that all of them had remained hidden during his walks and hunting excursions, as well across the centre as in the most out-of-the-way parts to the south? For Godfrey had never found a trace of them. Where was the mysterious den which vomited forth lions, hyænas, panthers, tigers? Amongst all the unaccountable things up to now this was indeed the most unaccountable.

Carefinotu could not believe what he heard. We have said that his astonishment was extreme. By the light of the fire which illuminated the interior of Will Tree there could be seen on his black face the strangest of grimaces.

Tartlet in the corner, groaned and lamented, and moaned

133

again. He would have asked Godfrey all about it, but Godfrey was not in the humour to reply. He had a presentiment of a very great danger, he was seeking for a way to retreat from it.

Once or twice Carefinotu and he went out to the centre of the palisade. They wished to see that the door was firmly and strongly shut.

Suddenly an avalanche of animals appeared with a huge tumult along the front of Will Tree.

It was only the goats and sheep and agouties. Terrified at the howling of the wild beasts, and scenting their approach, they had fled from their pasturage to take shelter behind the palisade.

"We must open the door!" exclaimed Godfrey.

Carefinotu nodded his head. He did not want to know the language to understand what Godfrey meant.

The door was opened, and the frightened flock rushed into the enclosure.

But at that instant there appeared through the opening a gleaming of eyes in the depths of the darkness which the shadow of the sequoias rendered still more profound.

There was no time to close the enclosure!

To jump at Godfrey, seize him in spite of himself, push him into the dwelling and slam the door, was done by Carefinotu like a flash of lightning.

New roarings indicated that three or four wild beasts had just cleared the palisade.

Then these horrible roarings were mingled with quite a concert of bleatings and groanings of terror. The domestic flock were taken as in a trap and delivered over to the clutches of the assailants.

Godfrey and Carefinotu, who had climbed up to the two small windows in the bark of the sequoia, endeavoured to see what was passing in the gloom.

Evidently the wild animals—tigers or lions, panthers or hyænas, they did not know which yet—had thrown themselves on the flock and begun their slaughter.

At this moment, Tartlet, in a paroxysm of blind terror, seized one of the muskets, and would have taken a chance shot out of one of the windows.

Godfrey stopped him.

"No!" said he. "In this darkness our shots will be lost, and we must not waste our ammunition! Wait for daylight!"

He was right. The bullets would just as likely have struck the domestic as the wild animals—more likely in fact, for the former

134

were the most numerous. To save them was now impossible. Once they were sacrificed, the wild beasts, thoroughly gorged, might quit the enclosure before sunrise. They would then see how to act to guard against a fresh invasion.

It was most important too, during the dark night, to avoid as much as possible revealing to these animals the presence of human beings, whom they might prefer to the flock. Perhaps they would thus avoid a direct attack against Will Tree.

As Tartlet was incapable of understanding either this reasoning or any other, Godfrey contented himself with depriving him of his weapon. The professor then went and threw himself on his bed and freely anathematized all travels and travellers and maniacs who could not remain quietly at their own firesides.

Both his companions resumed their observations at the windows.

Thence they beheld, without the power of interference, the horrible massacre which was taking place in the gloom. The cries of the sheep and the goats gradually diminished as the slaughter of the animals was consummated, although the greater part had escaped outside, where death, none the less certain, awaited them. This loss was irreparable for the little colony; but Godfrey was not then anxious about the future. The present was disquieting enough to occupy all his thoughts.

There was nothing they could do, nothing they could try, to hinder this work of destruction.

Godfrey and Carefinotu kept constant watch, and now they seemed to see new shadows coming up and passing into the palisade, while a fresh sound of footsteps struck on their ears.

Evidently certain belated beasts, attracted by the odour of the blood which impregnated the air, had traced the scent up to Will Tree.

They ran to and fro, they rushed round and round the tree and gave forth their hoarse and angry growls. Some of the shadows jumped on the ground like enormous cats. The slaughtered flock had not been sufficient to satisfy their rage.

Neither Godfrey nor his companions moved. In keeping completely motionless they might avoid a direct attack.

An unlucky shot suddenly revealed their presence and exposed them to the greatest danger.

Tartlet, a prey to a veritable hallucination, had risen. He had seized a revolver; and this time, before Godfrey and Carefinotu could hinder him, and not knowing himself what he did, but believing that he saw a tiger standing before him, he had fired! The bullet passed through the door of Will Tree.

"Fool!" exclaimed Godfrey, throwing himself on Tartlet, while the negro seized the weapon.

It was too late. The alarm was given, and growlings still more violent resounded without. Formidable talons were heard tearing the bark of the sequoia. Terrible blows shook the door, which was too feeble to resist such an assault.

"We must defend ourselves!" shouted Godfrey.

And, with his gun in his hand and his cartridge-pouch round his waist, he took his post at one of the windows.

To his great surprise, Carefinotu had done the same! Yes! the black, seizing the second musket—a weapon which he had never before handled—had filled his pockets with cartridges and taken his place at the second window.

Then the reports of the guns began to echo from the embrasures. By the flashes, Godfrey on the one side, and Carefinotu on the other, beheld the foes they had to deal with.

There, in the enclosure, roaring with rage, howling at the reports, rolling beneath the bullets which struck many of them, leapt of lions and tigers, and hyænas and panthers, at least a score. To their roarings and growlings which reverberated from afar, there echoed back those of other ferocious beasts running up to join them. Already the now distant roaring could be heard as they approached the environs of Will Tree. It was as though quite a menagerie of wild animals had been suddenly set free on the island!

However, Godfrey and Carefinotu, without troubling themselves about Tartlet, who could be of no use, were keeping as cool as they could, and refraining from firing unless they were certain of their aim. Wishing to waste not a shot, they waited till a shadow passed in front of them. Then came the flash and the report, and then a growl of grief told them that the animal had been hit.

A quarter of an hour elapsed, and then came a respite. Had the wild beasts given up the attack which had cost the lives of so many amongst them? Were they waiting for the day to recommence the attempt under more favourable conditions?

Whatever might be the reason, neither Godfrey nor Carefinotu desired to leave his post. The black had shown himself no less ready with the gun than Godfrey. If that was due only to the instinct of imitation, it must be admitted that it was indeed surprising.

About two o'clock in the morning there came a new alarm— more furious than before. The danger was imminent, the position in

136

the interior of Will Tree was becoming untenable. New growlings resounded round the foot of the sequoia. Neither Godfrey nor Carefinotu, on account of the situation of the windows, which were cut straight through, could see the assailants, nor, in consequence, could they fire with any chance of success.

It was now the door which the beasts attacked, and it was only too evident that it would be beaten in by their weight or torn down by their claws.

Godfrey and the black had descended to the ground. The door was already shaking beneath the blows from without. They could feel the heated breath making its way in through the cracks in the bark.

Godfrey and Carefinotu attempted to prop back the door with the stakes which kept up the beds, but these proved quite useless.

It was obvious that in a little while it would be driven in, for the beasts were mad with rage—particularly as no shots could reach them.

Godfrey was powerless. If he and his companions were inside Will Tree when the assailants broke in, their weapons would be useless to protect them.

Godfrey had crossed his arms. He saw the boards of the door open little by little. He could do nothing. In a moment of hesitation, he passed his hand across his forehead, as if in despair. But soon recovering his self-possession, he shouted,—

"Up we go! Up! All of us!"

And he pointed to the narrow passage which led up to the fork inside Will Tree.

Carefinotu and he, taking their muskets and revolvers, supplied themselves with cartridges.

And now he turned to make Tartlet follow them into these heights where he had never ventured before.

Tartlet was no longer there. He had started up while his companions were firing.

"Up!" repeated Godfrey.

It was a last retreat, where they would assuredly be sheltered from the wild beasts. If any tiger or panther attempted to come up into the branches of the sequoia, it would be easy to defend the hole through which he would have to pass.

Godfrey and Carefinotu had scarcely ascended thirty feet, when the roaring was heard in the interior of Will Tree. A few moments more and they would have been surprised. The door had just fallen in. They both hurried along, and at last reached the upper end of the hole.

A scream of terror welcomed them. It was Tartlet, who imagined he saw a panther or tiger! The unfortunate professor was clasping a branch, frightened almost out of his life lest he should fall.

Carefinotu went to him, and compelled him to lean against an upright bough, to which he firmly secured him with his belt.

Then, while Godfrey selected a place whence he could command the opening, Carefinotu went to another spot whence he could deliver a cross fire.

And they waited.

Under these circumstances it certainly looked as though the besieged were safe from attack.

Godfrey endeavoured to discover what was passing beneath them; but the night was still too dark. Then he tried to hear; and the growlings, which never ceased, showed that the assailants had no thought of abandoning the place.

Suddenly, towards four o'clock in the morning, a great light appeared at the foot of the tree. At once it shot out through the door and windows. At the same time a thick smoke spread forth from the upper opening and lost itself in the higher branches.

"What is that now?" exclaimed Godfrey.

It was easily explained. The wild beasts, in ravaging the interior of Will Tree, had scattered the remains of the fire. The fire had spread to the things in the room. The flame had caught the bark, which had dried and become combustible. The gigantic sequoia was ablaze below.

The position was now more terrible than it had ever been. By the light of the flames, which illuminated the space beneath the grove, they could see the wild beasts leaping round the foot of Will Tree.

At the same instant, a fearful explosion occurred. The sequoia, violently wrenched, trembled from its roots to its summit.

It was the reserve of gunpowder which had exploded inside Will Tree, and the air, violently expelled from the opening, rushed forth like the gas from a discharging cannon.

Godfrey and Carefinotu were almost torn from their resting-places. Had Tartlet not been lashed to the branch, he would assuredly have been hurled to the ground.

The wild beasts, terrified at the explosion, and more or less wounded, had taken to flight.

But at the same time the conflagration, fed by the sudden combustion of the powder, had considerably extended. It swiftly grew in dimensions as it crept up the enormous stem.

Large tongues of flame lapped the interior, and the highest soon reached the fork, and the dead wood snapped and crackled like shots from a revolver. A huge glare lighted up, not only the group of giant trees, but even the whole of the coast from Flag Point to the southern cape of Dream Bay.

Soon the fire had reached the lower branches of the sequoia, and threatened to invade the spot where Godfrey and his companions had taken refuge. Were they then to be devoured by the flames, with which they could not battle, or had they but the last resource of throwing themselves to the ground to escape being burnt alive? In either case they must die!

Godfrey sought about for some means of escape. He saw none!

Already the lower branches were ablaze and a dense smoke was struggling with the first gleams of dawn which were rising in the east.

At this moment there was a horrible crash of rending and breaking. The sequoia, burnt to the very roots, cracked violently—it toppled over—it fell!

But as it fell the stem met the stems of the trees which environed it; their powerful branches were mingled with its own, and so it remained obliquely cradled at an angle of about forty-five degrees from the ground.

At the moment that the sequoia fell, Godfrey and his companions believed themselves lost!

"Nineteenth of January!" exclaimed a voice, which Godfrey, in spite of his astonishment, immediately recognized.

It was Carefinotu! Yes, Carefinotu had just pronounced these words, and in that English language which up to then he had seemed unable to speak or to understand!

"What did you say?" asked Godfrey, as he followed him along the branches.

"I said, Mr. Morgan," answered Carefinotu, "that to-day your Uncle Will ought to reach us, and that if he doesn't turn up we are done for!"

139

CHAPTER XXII

WHICH CONCLUDES BY EXPLAINING WHAT UP TO NOW HAD APPEARED INEXPLICABLE

At that instant, and before Godfrey could reply, the report of fire-arms was heard not far from Will Tree.

At the same time one of those rain storms, regular cataracts in their fury, fell in a torrential shower just as the flames devouring the lower branches were threatening to seize upon the trees against which Will Tree was resting.

What was Godfrey to think after this series of inexplicable events? Carefinotu speaking English like a cockney, calling him by his name, announcing the early arrival of Uncle Will, and then the sudden report of the fire-arms?

He asked himself if he had gone mad; but he had no time for insoluble questions, for below him—hardly five minutes after the first sound of the guns—a body of sailors appeared hurrying through the trees.

Godfrey and Carefinotu slipped down along the stem, the interior of which was still burning.

But the moment that Godfrey touched the ground, he heard himself spoken to, and by two voices which even in his trouble it was impossible for him not to recognize.

"Nephew Godfrey, I have the honour to salute you!"

"Godfrey! Dear Godfrey!"

"Uncle Will! Phina! You!" exclaimed Godfrey, astounded.

Three seconds afterwards he was in somebody's arms, and was clasping that somebody in his own.

At the same time two sailors, at the order of Captain Turcott who was in command, climbed up along the sequoia to set Tartlet free, and, with all due respect, pluck him from the branch as if he were a fruit.

And then the questions, the answers, the explanations which passed!

"Uncle Will! You?"

"Yes! me!"

"And how did you discover Phina Island?"

"Phina Island!" answered William W. Kolderup. "You should say Spencer Island! Well, it wasn't very difficult. I bought it six months ago!"

"Spencer Island!"

"And you gave my name to it, you dear Godfrey!" said the young lady.

"The new name is a good one, and we will keep to it," answered the uncle; "but for geographers this is Spencer Island, only three days' journey from San Francisco, on which I thought it would be a good plan for you to serve your apprenticeship to the Crusoe business!"

"Oh! Uncle! Uncle Will! What is it you say?" exclaimed Godfrey. "Well, if you are in earnest, I can only answer that I deserved it! But then, Uncle Will, the wreck of the *Dream*?"

"Sham!" replied William W. Kolderup, who had never seemed in such a good humour before. "The *Dream* was quietly sunk by means of her water ballast, according to the instructions I had given Turcott. You thought she sank for good, but when the captain saw that you and Tartlet had got safely to land he brought her up and steamed away. Three days later he got back to San Francisco, and he it is who has brought us to Spencer Island on the date we fixed!"

"Then none of the crew perished in the wreck?"

"None—unless it was the unhappy Chinaman who hid himself away on board and could not be found!"

"But the canoe?"

"Sham! The canoe was of my own make."

"But the savages?"

"Sham! The savages whom luckily you did not shoot!"

"But Carefinotu?"

"Sham! Carefinotu was my faithful Jup Brass, who played his part of Friday marvellously well, as I see."

"Yes," answered Godfrey. "He twice saved my life—once from a bear, once from a tiger—"

"The bear was sham! the tiger was sham!" laughed William W. Kolderup. "Both of them were stuffed with straw, and landed before you saw them with Jup Brass and his companions!"

"But he moved his head and his paws!"

"By means of a spring which Jup Brass had fixed during the night a few hours before the meetings which were prepared for you."

"What! all of them?" repeated Godfrey, a little ashamed at having been taken in by these artifices.

"Yes! Things were going too smoothly in your island, and we had to get up a little excitement!"

"Then," answered Godfrey, who had begun to laugh, "if you

141

wished to make matters unpleasant for us, why did you send us the box which contained everything we wanted?"

"A box?" answered William W. Kolderup. "What box? I never sent you a box! Perhaps by chance—"

And as he said so he looked towards Phina, who cast down her eyes and turned away her head.

"Oh! indeed!—a box! but then Phina must have had an accomplice—"

And Uncle Will turned towards Captain Turcott, who laughingly answered,—

"What could I do, Mr. Kolderup? I can sometimes resist you— but Miss Phina—it was too difficult! And four months ago, when you sent me to look round the island, I landed the box from my boat—"

"Dearest Phina!" said Godfrey, seizing the young lady's hand.

"Turcott, you promised to keep the secret!" said Phina with a blush.

And Uncle William W. Kolderup, shaking his big head, tried in vain to hide that he was touched.

But if Godfrey could not restrain his smiles as he listened to the explanations of Uncle Will, Professor Tartlet did not laugh in the least! He was excessively mortified at what he heard! To have been the object of such a mystification, he, a professor of dancing and deportment! And so advancing with much dignity he observed,—

"Mr. William Kolderup will hardly assert, I imagine, that the enormous crocodile, of which I was nearly the unhappy victim, was made of pasteboard and wound up with a spring?"

"A crocodile?" replied the uncle.

"Yes, Mr. Kolderup," said Carefinotu, to whom we had better return his proper name of Jup Brass. "Yes, a real live crocodile, which went for Mr. Tartlet, and which I did not have in my collection!"

Godfrey then related what had happened, the sudden appearance of the wild beasts in such numbers, real lions, real tigers, real panthers, and then the invasion of the snakes, of which during four months they had not seen a single specimen in the island!

William W. Kolderup at this was quite disconcerted. He knew nothing about it. Spencer Island—it had been known for a long time—never had any wild beasts, did not possess even a single noxious animal; it was so stated in the deeds of sale.

Neither did he understand what Godfrey told him of the attempts he had made to discover the origin of the smoke which had appeared at different points on the island. And he seemed very much troubled to find that all had not passed on the island according to his instructions, and that the programme had been seriously interfered with.

As for Tartlet, he was not the sort of man to be humbugged. For his part he would admit nothing, neither the sham shipwreck, nor the sham savages, nor the sham animals, and above all he would never give up the glory which he had gained in shooting with the first shot from his gun the chief of the Polynesian tribe—one of the servants of the Kolderup establishment, who turned out to be as well as he was.

All was described, all was explained, except the serious matter of the real wild beasts and the unknown smoke. Uncle Will became very thoughtful about this. But, like a practical man, he put off, by an effort of the will, the solution of the problems, and addressing his nephew,—

"Godfrey," said he, "you have always been so fond of islands, that I am sure it will please you to hear that this is yours—wholly yours! I make you a present of it! You can do what you like with it! I never dreamt of bringing you away by force; and I would not take you away from it! Be then a Crusoe for the rest of your life, if your heart tells you to—"

"I!" answered Godfrey. "I! All my life!"

Phina stepped forward.

"Godfrey," she asked, "would you like to remain on your island?"

"I would rather die!" he exclaimed.

But immediately he added, as he took the young lady's hand,—

"Well, yes, I will remain; but on three conditions. The first is, you stay with me, dearest Phina; the second is, that Uncle Will lives with us; and the third is, that the chaplain of the *Dream* marries us this very day!"

"There is no chaplain on board the *Dream*, Godfrey!" replied Uncle Will. "You know that very well. But I think there is still one left in San Francisco, and that we can find some worthy minister to perform the service! I believe I read your thoughts when I say that before to-morrow we shall put to sea again!"

Then Phina and Uncle Will asked Godfrey to do the honours of his island. Behold them then walking under the group of sequoias, along the stream up to the little bridge.

Alas! of the habitation at Will Tree nothing remained. The fire had completely devoured the dwelling in the base of the tree! Without the arrival of William W. Kolderup, what with the

143

approaching winter, the destruction of their stores, and the genuine wild beasts in the island, our Crusoes would have deserved to be pitied.

"Uncle Will!" said Godfrey. "If I gave the island the name of Phina, let me add that I gave our dwelling the name of Will Tree!"

"Well," answered the uncle, "we will take away some of the seed, and plant it in my garden at 'Frisco!"

During the walk they noticed some wild animals in the distance; but they dared not attack so formidable a party as the sailors of the *Dream*. But none the less was their presence absolutely incomprehensible.

Then they returned on board, not without Tartlet asking permission to bring off "his crocodile"—a permission which was granted.

That evening the party were united in the saloon of the *Dream*, and there was quite a cheerful dinner to celebrate the end of the adventures of Godfrey Morgan and his marriage with Phina Hollaney.

On the morrow, the 20th of January, the *Dream* set sail under the command of Captain Turcott. At eight o'clock in the morning Godfrey, not without emotion, saw the horizon in the west wipe out, as if it were a shadow, the island on which he had been to school for six months—a school of which he never forgot the lessons.

The passage was rapid; the sea magnificent; the wind favourable. This time the *Dream* went straight to her destination! There was no one to be mystified! She made no tackings without number as on the first voyage! She did not lose during the night what she had gained during the day!

And so on the 23rd of January, after passing at noon through the Golden Gate, she entered the vast bay of San Francisco, and came alongside the wharf in Merchant Street.

And what did they then see?

They saw issue from the hold a man who, having swum to the *Dream* during the night while she was anchored at Phina Island, had succeeded in stowing himself away for the second time!

And who was this man?

It was the Chinaman, Seng Vou, who had made the passage back as he had made the passage out!

Seng Vou advanced towards William W. Kolderup.

"I hope Mr. Kolderup will pardon me," said he very politely. "When I took my passage in the *Dream*, I thought she was going direct to Shanghai, and then I should have reached my country, but I leave her now, and return to San Francisco."

144

Every one, astounded at the apparition, knew not what to answer, and laughingly gazed at the intruder.

"But," said William W. Kolderup at last, "you have not remained six months in the hold, I suppose?"

"No!" answered Seng Vou.

"Where have you been, then?"

"On the island!"

"You!" exclaimed Godfrey.

"Yes."

"Then the smoke?"

"A man must have a fire!"

"And you did not attempt to come to us, to share our living?"

"A Chinaman likes to live alone," quietly replied Seng Vou. "He is sufficient for himself, and he wants no one!"

And thereupon this eccentric individual bowed to William W. Kolderup, landed, and disappeared.

"That is the stuff they make real Crusoes of!" observed Uncle Will. "Look at him and see if you are like him! It does not matter, the English race would do no good by absorbing fellows of that stamp!"

"Good!" said Godfrey, "the smoke is explained by the presence of Seng Vou; but the beasts?"

"And my crocodile!" added Tartlet; "I should like some one to explain my crocodile!"

William W. Kolderup seemed much embarrassed, and feeling in turn quite mystified, passed his hand over his forehead as if to clear the clouds away.

"We shall know later on," he said. "Everything is found by him who knows how to seek!"

A few days afterwards there was celebrated with great pomp the wedding of the nephew and pupil of William W. Kolderup. That the young couple were made much of by all the friends of the wealthy merchant can easily be imagined.

At the ceremony Tartlet was perfect in bearing, in everything, and the pupil did honour to the celebrated professor of dancing and deportment.

Now Tartlet had an idea. Not being able to mount his crocodile on a scarf-pin—and much he regretted it—he resolved to have it stuffed. The animal prepared in this fashion—hung from the ceiling, with the jaws half open, and the paws outspread—would make a fine ornament for his room. The crocodile was consequently sent to a famous taxidermist, and he brought it back to Tartlet a few

145

days afterwards. Every one came to admire the monster who had almost made a meal of Tartlet.

"You know, Mr. Kolderup, where the animal came from?" said the celebrated taxidermist, presenting his bill.

"No, I do not," answered Uncle Will.

"But it had a label underneath its carapace."

"A label!" exclaimed Godfrey.

"Here it is," said the celebrated taxidermist.

And he held out a piece of leather on which, in indelible ink, were written these words,—

"From Hagenbeck, Hamburg,
"To J. R. Taskinar, Stockton, U.S.A."

When William W. Kolderup had read these words he burst into a shout of laughter. He understood all.

It was his enemy, J. R. Taskinar, his conquered competitor, who, to be revenged, had bought a cargo of wild beasts, reptiles, and other objectionable creatures from a well-known purveyor to the menageries of both hemispheres, and had landed them at night in several voyages to Spencer Island. It had cost him a good deal, no doubt, to do so; but he had succeeded in infesting the property of his rival, as the English did Martinique, if we are to believe the legend, before it was handed over to France.

There was thus no more to explain of the remarkable occurrences on Phina Island.

"Well done!" exclaimed William W. Kolderup. "I could not have done better myself!"

"But with those terrible creatures," said Phina, "Spencer Island—"

"Phina Island—" interrupted Godfrey.

"Phina Island," continued the bride, with a smile, "is quite uninhabitable."

"Bah!" answered Uncle Will; "we can wait till the last lion has eaten up the last tiger!"

"And then, dearest Phina," said Godfrey, "you will not be afraid to pass a season there with me?"

"With you, my dear husband, I fear nothing from anywhere," answered Phina, "and as you have not had your voyage round the world—"

"We will have it together," said Godfrey, "and if an unlucky chance should ever make me a real Crusoe—"

146

"You will ever have near you the most devoted of Crusoe-esses!"

THE END